VINNY’S WILDERNESS

First published in 2016 by Liberties Press
140 Terenure Road North | Terenure | Dublin 6W
T: +353 (1) 405 5701 | E: info@libertiespress.com |
W: libertiespress.com

Trade enquiries to Gill
Hume Avenue | Park West | Dublin 12
T: +353 (1) 500 9534 | F: +353 (1) 500 9595 |
E: sales@gillmacmillan.ie

Distributed in the United Kingdom by Turnaround Publisher Services
Unit 3 | Olympia Trading Estate | Coburg Road | London N22 6TZ
T: +44 (0) 20 8829 3000 | E: orders@turnaround-uk.com

Distributed in the United States by Casemate-IPM
22841 Quicksilver Dr | Dulles, VA 20166
T: +1 (703) 661-1586 | F: +1 (703) 661-1547 |
E: ipmmail@presswarehouse.com

ISBN: 978-1-910742-34-1
2 4 6 8 10 9 7 5 3 1

A CIP record for this title is available from the British Library.
Cover design by Liberties Press
Internal design by Liberties Press

The publishers gratefully acknowledge the
financial assistance of the Arts Council of Northern Ireland.

VINNY'S WILDERNESS

Janet Shepperson

To the children from all the schools I've worked in over the years.

You are all adults now, but when you were kids,

you taught me so much.

Contents

MONDAY 15 JUNE

On the top deck of the bus, Vinny sits with the grey-mauve sky lulling her to sleep. A soft evening, as they say in the country: the promise of more rain.

Then her phone tings. A tiny, unsettling sound, a text or an e-mail. *Pay attention to me*, it says, *I could be an emergency. Your daughter's home alone isn't she, for the first time ever? And you spent half the staff meeting worrying about her?*

The phone is in her bag, underneath another bag full of stories to mark, all settled on the seat beside her. Why spend her last few minutes of peace and quiet ferreting about for what'll only turn out to be some stupid e-mail about renewing her house insurance, or the contents of her garden, or some such nonsense? Besides, she'll be home in five minutes, and Roisin's nearly eleven; she'd said if there were any problems, she'd go next door.

But even while she's thinking this, her hands are automatically shifting stuff about, and pulling out the phone. It's a text. It's incomprehensible.

> No more mess and muddle for Lavinia, whether or not it is 'creative'.

There's a number at the top that she doesn't recognise. Who is this person, and how did he get her number? Because it's definitely a *he*, there's something faintly bossy, unmistakably masculine. And chilling. Is it some kind of threat? Or is it just a crank? Or some colleague from the school, playing some kind of weird joke? But who calls her Lavinia? That in itself seems quite threatening.

Her stomach is tying itself in a knot. The bus lurches to a halt, she struggles to her feet, she's nearly missed her stop, she gathers her belongings in an awkward heap clutched against her chest, using her free arm to swing herself down the stairs.

Vinny's heart always lifts when she gets off the bus. Because it all worked out so beautifully, when she was skint and didn't want to take Rory's money; everybody said, 'You can get a really cheap house up in North Belfast, if you're not too fussy about what sort of area you live in.' But she was fussy, she held out until she found this place. Leafyland, the outer fringes of South Belfast, a mixed area, a modest but decent little terrace, no sectarian flags, and she and Roisin have the end house with all that lovely garden.

And here at the bus stop is Roisin, hair all ruffled, face as pink as a baby about to start bawling, tears, real tears streaking down.

'What's wrong, *mo chara*?'

'Mum! Mum! It's the garden!'

'What's in the garden?'

'It's gone, they're taking it, they're stealing it—'

'Calm down, pet, tell me what happened, you should have phoned me—'

Roisin stamps her foot in exasperation.

'I couldn't! They were out there and I couldn't find my phone and they were tearing the place to bits and I couldn't phone you—'

Vinny takes hold of both shoulders and stares at her.

'Now. Do you remember, I told you not to answer the door?'

Roisin glares at her.

'It's not my fault! They never came to the door, by the time I got home they were already out there, in the garden!'

Vinny grabs hold of her hand and they start walking fast, the bags of books bumping against Vinny's free side.

'Nobody said it was your fault, pet, now tell me—'

'When I was coming up the street I could hear this roaring noise, and I went in the house and looked out the back window and there was a digger, actually a digger in the garden – and then I couldn't find my phone—'

Yes, Vinny thinks. *There's no fence in the front,*

and it's all open at the side, so yes, a digger could get round – but why on earth—

As soon as they turn into the street, she sees the skip. It's enormous. It's piled high with earth and what looks like rubble, this can't be from her garden, there isn't any rubble in her garden. It must be from someone else's.

There's vegetation poking out. All clogged up with earth. As they get nearer, she recognises it: sweet amber. Straggly, reddish twigs and little green leaves blushing to red, and red berries already turning black. She can smell its soft, fruity scent. It only gives off that scent if you touch or disturb it. How often has she sat on the raised stone terrace on a summer evening, drinking her coffee, watching Roisin and her friends playing hide-and-seek? And every time they brush against it, it gives off that marvellous scent.

She walks up to the skip, leans in, gathers the straggly twigs in the arms and buries her face in them. This is her sweet amber. She knows it is. Something appalling has happened.

She dumps her bags on the doorstep. She and Roisin go into the kitchen but they can only see half the back garden, because someone has turned the trampoline over on its side, and it is leaning up against the window, blocking the patio doors. So she can't get out there, she's trapped inside with the roaring and an indistinct view of figures disappearing and re-appearing on the other side of a large black circle. In the face of her mother's helplessness, Roisin's tears are welling up again.

Back out the front they go, ready to charge round the side into the garden, make that awful machine stop. But out here in the street there's more noise: a lorry drawing up opposite. '*21ST CENTURY LANDSCAPING*', is written in capitals across the side. Ice-green, Vinny thinks, if there is such a colour.

In the back, plants. These plants are not clogged with earth or squashed by rubble. They stand up proud, complacent and slightly ridiculous. The young trees, with their fragile branches and leaves clinging tentatively, they don't look too bad, but the pampas grass, huge overblown white tassels that look like 1980s interior decoration gone mad, they look so incongruous . . . even in the middle of her shock and confusion, their pomposity makes Vinny want to laugh.

Two men jump down from the lorry. One starts unloading a pile of off-white paving stones, tossing them down as casually as if they were polystyrene. The other advances towards her with a folder.

'Mrs Corcoran?'

'Yes.'

'These're your plans, missis. It's all in here, a wee map and care and maintenance instructions, and detailed costings. Nothing cheap. He's ordered you the best of everything.'

'He?'

'Your husband.'

'I don't have a husband,' she says weakly.

'Aye, well, that's nothing to do with us . . . '

'I don't know anything about this,' she protests.

'That's right, he said he wanted to surprise you. We gave him the estimate over the phone, he didn't want to let on till the stuff was actually delivered. Oh, and he asked us to give you this.'

It's an orchid, off-white, the same colour as the paving stones and the pampas grass, in a shiny pot, wrapped in polythene. Roisin, coming up behind her, says 'That's hideous,' and it's true. This is the ugliest orchid Vinny has ever seen.

'Roisin, go in and look for your phone again,' she tells her firmly. 'I'll be in in five minutes, we'll find it, I promise. I'll just get this sorted out first.'

'If you could maybe show us exactly where you want the flowering cherry trees . . . ' the man is saying, and she follows him, wordlessly, round into the back garden.

She cannot believe the extent of the devastation. It's a wilderness of churned-up earth, churned up, but flat. All the little bumpy bits are gone, and what's happened to the wee raised stone terrace? Is that what the rubble in the skip is – smashed up fragments of what's served Roisin and her friends so often as a play house, a pretend school, a pirate ship, an aeroplane, a castle?

The digger has rumbled to a halt, but the man is still talking.

'Shame really, you had a couple of nice standards, but he said all those apples falling on the lawn made it look messy, he said you wanted the whole thing done over . . . '

'Who said?'

He looks baffled.

'Isn't there a name on the card?'

Vinny is still clutching the wretched orchid. She peels back the polythene and pulls out a small white card, with the '*21ST CENTURY LANDSCAPING*' logo in one corner. She can't believe it. The message is exactly the same as that text; but this time it's signed.

> No more mess or muddle for Lavinia, whether or not it is 'creative'.
>
> Derek Masterton

Derek. With his eyes grey and sharp as gravel. His cautious, giving-nothing-away expression. His perfectly groomed salt-and-pepper hair, his unobtrusively expensive jackets that always look fresh from the dry cleaners, his thinly striped shirts with cufflinks, actual cufflinks. Derek, who had surely never done a spontaneous thing in his life.

She tries to speak but nothing comes out. Finally the man notices.

'Em . . . right. You look a wee bit stunned? Right enough it looks a mess now, but wait'll you see . . . there's lots of good stuff here . . . '

A light rain is beginning to fall. Vinny shivers.

'It's like the surface of the moon'

'Ach it'll be fine when it's all planted up, you've lots of lovely heathers and ornamental shrubs, and you've white gravel round the flowering trees, it'll be nice and bright . . . '

'White gravel?'

'And some artificial turf, that'll never get muddy.'

'Artificial turf?'

'If you look at the plans . . . '

She puts down the wretched orchid, with its waspish little note, on a damp bit of stone that seems to have escaped the attention of the digger. It's all that's left of the crooked path that used to cross her wild lawn.

Wordlessly she takes the folder the man is offering her, but she doesn't look at it. The rain is falling steadily now. Everything round her is turning to mud, gleaming with a sort of evil sheen. Fifty shades of brown. She realises it's hardly rained for weeks; with all that's been going on, she's hardly had time to notice how dry and prickly everything's been getting. She goes back into the house, where she can't see the devastation. Closes her eyes, leans against a pillar. There's a faint smell of lavender which she'd dried and hung up last summer, dusty and a bit cobwebby but still giving off a slight fragrance when you lean against it.

She tries to summon up images of what she's lost, but here's Roisin still gurning about her phone. She hands over her own mobile.

'Ring your number.'

'What?'

'Ring it!'

The ringtone fizzing across the kitchen reveals Roisin's phone underneath her homework notebook, on the kitchen table. Roisin snatches it up triumphantly. But then a text from her friend Zoe plunges her into further misery.

'Mum, Zoe says can she bring her friend Tasha to my birthday? Mum, what about my birthday? It's only two and a half weeks away and we were supposed to have a bouncy castle and do the high ropes course in the garden?'

Vinny hugs her. It's meant to be a bracing hug, but it feels more like a desperate clutch.

'Go upstairs. Turn on the computer. Look up Indianaland, Laser Quest, all those place your friends have had parties at.'

'But I thought it was too expensive?'

'Well, suddenly it isn't. We can go up to £100. Find out how much they charge per head, write it all down for me, make a list of the different places so we can compare—'

Roisin hasn't smiled since Vinny got off the bus. Now she gives a big, disbelieving grin and pounds off up the stairs. Vinny hears the musical sigh the computer makes when you switch it on. She closes her eyes again. Hears an embarrassed cough. Opens them. The man is standing in her front doorway, framed by the grey suburban rain, looking at her nervously. He must think she's loopy, because what can she mean by saying she doesn't have a husband? She must have a husband, or at least a fairly well-off partner, because otherwise who's paying for all this?

He says, 'We're off now, missis.'

'You're leaving?'

'Can't do anything more till it stops raining. We'll be back in the morning, half past eight. Providing the rain's stopped. You should maybe take a look at those plans? If there's anything you want done different, we can change it, you know? Maybe you should have a wee word with, er, him?'

'Of course,' Vinny says.

The man goes. She sits down at the table. A wee word. Him. The phone with its small black screen in front of her, hiding the baffling text. So smooth. So hostile.

She tries to think clearly, but she's overwhelmed by a jumble of remembered images. Brambles, buddleia, flowering currant. Silvery branches of the dead rowan tree, poking up from a mass of ivy, its glossy leaves like a forest, a waterfall, a spiky green wave. Places for cats to crouch and wrens to scold them. All that luxuriant growth and decay: anarchy, fecundity, creativity. Her wild garden where she used to sit gazing at the speckled wood butterflies, the bees pottering in and out of the foxgloves, right through from the chilly days of April to the last golden days of October. Gone. All of it. Gone.

She remembers Roisin, a chubby three year old when they first moved in, in full flight from a sour, failed marriage. Roisin, missing her daddy, but consoled by all the new things she could do in this wilderness: stalk the neighbours' cats, feed her dolls on real blackberries, play hide-and-seek with her mum in the huge, straggly rhododendron. Usually Roisin was quite visible behind its convoluted branches, but Vinny was always good at pretending.

She can send away all that stupid stuff – the ornamental heathers, the ridiculous pampas grass, the white gravel. But she can never get back that ancient rhododendron. The apple tree, all covered in lichen, with its makeshift swing. The dead rowan swamped with ivy, leaves dark green and glossy all year round, wood pigeons pecking importantly at the berries, their ponderous pink-and-grey plumpness somehow reminding her of characters from the Beatrix Potter books she read to Roisin. 'We don't have Jemima Puddleduck,' she used to say, 'but we do have Jemima Pigeon, she's nearly as big as a duck . . .'

She gets up and goes to the sink to fill the kettle and is transfixed all over again by the sight of a waste land of churned-up mud. It's only June now. How many summer evenings is she going to have to stay indoors, ignoring the desolation? How will she cope in October, her thoughts full of the ghosts of tawny crumpled leaves and bird-pecked windfall apples and cat paths across the dewy autumn grass?

Her phone tings again. If this is another text from Derek, she's going to hurl the damn thing into the bin. But it's not. It's a text from Alex. Her thumbnail photo gleams on Vinny's phone, just as she always gleams for the camera, as if her life's one long photo shoot.

No word from her all day yesterday, and now this.

> Vinny I'm so, so sorry. I just honestly can't believe it. Never thought he'd do a thing like that. It's mental. Just had to get away, I'm up here in Portrush, skype soon, tell you everything. Xxx

Not a word about her wee fella's tutoring session with Vinny, which is due to start – she checks her watch – in twenty minutes. What the hell is she doing up in Portrush?

And what is 'everything'? Have she and that weaselly Derek been discussing her, and the wild chaotic garden, and what could be done, and did they cook up some awful plan together, involving ornamental heathers and white gravel?

It's impossible, she thinks. Alex and Derek were barely speaking. In fact, they weren't. Anyway, Alex knows I love that garden, mess and all, it's the one place I have to retreat to when everything else goes wrong, Alex would never . . . Alex is my friend . . . Besides, the words 'Alex' and 'Derek' and 'together' don't really belong in the same sentence. But how did Derek get my phone number?

With the rain lashing down outside and the upturned trampoline blocking most of the light from the windows, the kitchen is as dark as a winter's day. She stirs her coffee; her mobile phone is a little point of light.

She scrolls back through Alex's texts. Breathless little scraps of chat, jokes, arrangements, apologies . . . spelling pretty off the wall . . . cheerful, insouciant, shiny. She hadn't realised how much they'd texted each other. Almost every day for the last two months. Reading this stuff, you'd think they were best friends, inseparable. And she'd forgotten how gushing Alex could be. Look at this one: 'I guess you're right, you always say such wise things.' And, even a couple of weeks ago, 'So glad I found you again.'

'Oh, you're glad, are you?' Vinny snarls.

She realises she's spoken aloud. Could Roisin hear her from upstairs? She listens. She can hear Roisin's excited voice, then a pause, then more excited chatter. The words 'Laser' and 'Paintball'. She shudders. Anyway, Roisin's happy, for the moment, for half an hour at least, maybe even an hour. Roisin can talk to her friends for an interminability, if Vinny doesn't cut her off by scolding about the expense.

She tips the undrunk coffee down the sink and pours herself a glass of wine from one of the bottles left over from her disastrous attempt at a party. It's gone sour. *Hell*, she thinks, *it doesn't matter what it tastes like, I'm going to do an Alex here: I'm going to drink to slow down, to calm down, to make myself stay sitting down . . .*

She goes across to the lounge area. She settles on the sofa, cross-legged, her back to the kitchen window so that she can't see the hideous, rain-soaked gash in her life. She shivers. Takes the bright green throw off the back of the sofa and wraps it round her shoulders.

Her phone tings again. It has to be Alex, doesn't it? The message simply says,

Skype now? X

This time she actually does throw the phone. Not into the bin, but into the empty fireplace. It clangs against the metal bars of the grate and comes to rest amongst the fir cones which she'd so carefully arranged the day before the party. Let it ting all it likes, she won't answer it.

She will not speak to Alex, she wishes she'd never met Alex. This is all her fault. They were happy enough, her and Roisin, till Alex came along. She's sick of worrying about Alex's problems. Her and that smooth, tight-arsed weasel of a husband. Oh, she complains about him, and the struggles of her life, but really, hasn't she got everything she always wanted? And if there's anything she hasn't got, he'll buy it for her. Including tutoring for her gormless wee fella . . . or maybe, as a last resort, a boarding place at some posh school where the hoods and flag protesters can't get in. And anything, anything can be bought. Except for Vinny's wilderness, that was irreplaceable. She can never buy another one.

Her phone tings again. No, she thinks, I will not go on Skype and start screaming and shouting at her. I will not pace about the room and throw my mobile and punch the cushions. I will just sit here, me and my glass of sour wine, and I'll do my grieving. That *indwelling* thing people do, when somebody dies. I'll go over and over the garden in my mind, till the pictures start to fade. Maybe I'll have a bit of a cry. Then I'll let it go.

She closes her eyes and waits for an image of the bright, tangled garden to swim up, maybe with some apples tumbled on the lawn, or Roisin on the swing? But her eyes keep popping open. It's the front garden she sees: the only bit of garden that's survived. Scrubby grass, primulas along the weed-grown path, this is spring she's remembering, and Alex coming up to her open front door, stiffly poised, alert, a bit defiant.

She closes her eyes again. Buries her face in a cushion. In the warm, scratchy, sour-wine-smelling darkness, the last four months unroll like a film. She's astonished at the vividness of her memories. She can almost smell the stew she was cooking when the doorbell rang, almost feel the brisk spring wind tugging at her hair as she stood on the doorstep. She can hear an ice-cream van in the distance, and a dog barking two doors down, and Alex's silvery voice with its carefully constructed Malone Road accent, gushing nervously.

MARCH

The first thing she said to me was, 'My husband's starting to get anxious. He says it's high time we did something about him. Wee Denzil.'

'Oh,' I said. 'You're the woman who phoned? Mrs Masterton?'

'Oh, just call me Alex.'

'Right. I'm Vinny Corcoran.'

'I know,' she said, in a slightly odd voice.

Then there was that whole shaking hands thing which I usually hate, because some parents expect it and some don't, you can be left clutching limp fingers or a couple of bangles or even a bit of sleeve. But Alex – although she did have bangles, gleaming and expensive-looking, jangling together – gave me a firm, practised handshake. Just a little twist of her mouth, though, as if she'd bitten down on something unexpectedly sour. A bit of lemon, or an olive.

The kitchen was a tip, and with the whole thing being open plan, there was nowhere to hide the mess. So I brought her out into the garden, then realised what a shambles *that* must appear, seen through her eyes. With their fringe of beautifully groomed lashes, subtle eyeshadow shading from bronze to grey, elegantly arched eyebrows and carefully organised blonde-but-not-too-blonde hair. She couldn't have been more different from wee Johnny McAfee's mum – earnest and clumsy and sort of hopelessly ungroomed – she always put me in mind of one of those dogs that flop about advertising paint, so that I'll forever think of her as a Dulux dog, only without the TV stylists; a bit unkempt, cuddly but rather defeated-looking. Whereas, Alex had that greyhound-straining-at-the-leash quality. Greyhound, because she was sleek and streamlined and not an ounce of spare flesh on her anywhere. Straining, because she seemed so on edge, like at any moment a hare would appear and she'd be expected to chase it, and not only that, beat all the others to it.

Even the stone terrace I led her out to seemed to have grown more moss and weeds since the last time I looked at it, and the tangled shrubbery behind it was a mess, and could those be brambles poking their ignorant snouts out of the wilderness, right across one of the garden chairs?

At least the chairs weren't damp. I dragged them round to face the flowering currant, which was just coming into blossom, dark pink dangly flowers looking wild and charming, like a wee notelet card. She could sit and look at that while I got her a cup of tea.

'No thanks,' she said, 'I haven't got time.'

That probably wasn't meant to sound as haughty as it did.

'So,' I began, 'tell me about your wee fella.'

'Denzil, well, he's a good kid really, but he's always struggled. He just finds it really hard to concentrate, not like the other two.'

She started telling me about them. Stewart who was at Queen's and Chloe who was working really hard for her A levels, uncannily hard in fact, it was dizzying to watch her, and of course they were both going to be doctors, they'd always been so competitive, only two years between them, and of course it really helped them to focus . . . and when they were Denzil's age, they had no eleven-plus coaching at all. All the others had coaching even though it was a prep school, but Stewart and Chloe were already top of their classes practically all the time, so what would have been the point?

And all the time she was sitting rigid, her back not touching the back of the plastic chair, and every time she said 'Of course' she gave one of her copper bangles a twist and it clashed against the other one.

'Yes,' I said firmly, 'but tell me about Denzil, what sort of kid is he, what does he like doing?'

'Well . . . he loves the Cubs. He's mad keen about moving up to Scouts soon. He likes being outside, climbing things, running about, getting muddy, you know, regular wee boy . . . ach, he's a wee dote, really.'

At this point, her back finally made contact with the chair back and her feet came forward and stretched out a bit, and her mouth relaxed with a little puff as if she'd finally spat out the lemon.

'He's done more than a dozen badges. He's actually quite patient really, once he gets into something. He's even done Birdwatcher, he had to make a list of all the birds that come into our back garden, he'd sit and watch them for ages. See that wee thing jooking about in the tree? He could probably tell you what sort of bird that is.'

'It's a blue tit.'

'Oh. Well maybe he wouldn't want to tell you *that* . . . '

'So,' I continued, 'how does he feel about having a tutor?'

The mouth pursed up again and the feet snapped back under her.

'Well to be honest, we did try an agency. And he just would not co-operate *at all*. The tutor was a very humourless, strict sort of man and he completely rubbed Denzil up the wrong way, anyway Denzil was apparently quite disruptive, which isn't like him at *all*, he's normally such a placid, dreamy wee soul.'

She let out an exasperated sound, halfway between a snort and a sigh. She stared at Roisin, who'd come out and started rhythmically whacking a tennis ball on the back wall of the house, ignoring us. Roisin had come to terms with me tutoring one kid for the eleven-plus, or at least I thought she had, but the onset of another one was unsettling for her. She wanted to know why it was so important for *them* to pass the eleven-plus, when *she* wasn't even doing it? 'Because you're going to the integrated school,' I kept explaining. 'Well,' she'd ask, 'why don't they go there too?' 'Because not everybody can go to the integrated school, Roisin.'

'Also,' Alex said, 'he's a June birthday. Isn't that supposed to make it harder for them?'

'Yes, if he found it hard to settle at school when he was only just four. Did he?'

'Goodness, I can hardly remember. There was so much going on. Chloe was in first year at Methody, she needed an awful lot of input, and Stewart was choosing his GCSEs, and he didn't want to do three sciences and my husband said he'd really need to, for medicine, there was a lot of conflict and I guess I didn't pay much attention to wee Denzil . . . I was just glad he seemed to be having fun . . . '

Then she suddenly shrieked 'Denzil!' and there he was, standing in the kitchen doorway.

'I told you to stay in the car,' she scolded.

'I didn't have anything to do,' he explained calmly. 'My Nintendo needs recharging.'
He was gazing around at the big rhododendron and the three dilapidated trees and I could see him thinking, *Wow, an adventure playground!*

So I just took charge, instructing Denzil to explore the garden, hustling Alex Masterton into the shambles of my kitchen, embarrassing and all as it was, while I made her some coffee. We agreed that he'd come every Tuesday after school for an hour, and every Saturday at ten for an hour, and that I'd start off very gently so as to build up his confidence after the bad experience with the tutoring agency. I had to keep shoo-ing Roisin out, and I said 'You know, we really should have done all this on the phone,' and Alex glanced round at the shabby furniture and the dishes in the sink and Roisin's half-painted Viking ship made from cereal boxes and said in an almost neutral tone, 'I just wanted to see where you live.' There was something hovering in her voice and of course I couldn't understand, then, what it was.

Another shriek: this time it was Roisin, bursting in to say Denzil was on the roof. We rushed out and of course he wasn't on the house roof, just the roof of what the previous owners had grandly called the car port, actually a sheet of corrugated Perspex supported by a couple of iron poles, which you wouldn't think any kid could possibly have climbed. But it turned out he'd climbed up the dead rowan tree, with its mass of ivy that overhangs the car port, and sort of scrambled across.

'Denzil!' his mum roared. 'Get down this minute – watch what you're doing – that tree's not safe, them branches is ratten—'

Or did I just imagine that? A sudden twang of Belfast working class accent? Was she putting it on, trying to get a bit of humour out of the situation, or had the panic brought out something she usually kept well hidden?

Anyhow, she waded into the ivy, stood ready to catch him if he fell, and when he got safely down to the ground again, she brushed bits of greenery off him and he pretended to duck. I could see they had a rapport. I thought, *Well, at least this pair have a good relationship*. There's nothing worse than tutoring a kid who's at daggers drawn with both his parents.

Also, I really needed the money.

So I said 'OK, Saturday mornings for an hour and Tuesdays after school for an hour, how about that Denzil, unless you've already got something after school on Tuesdays?'

You have to honour their commitments; it doesn't help them relax and concentrate if they think that you think that the eleven-plus, or the AQA, as we're supposed to call it now, is the most important thing in the entire universe.

And he said, 'They're starting up extra rugby for P6 boys, I'm supposed to go to it, but I don't like it.'

His mum laughed and ruffled his hair.

'Hasn't got a competitive bone in his body, have you, son?'

He shook his head and grinned at her. She turned to Roisin, who was standing with a protective hand on the ivy-clad tree trunk.

'So, what's it like having your mum as your teacher?'

'Oh, she's not *my* teacher,' Roisin said stiffly. 'She's P7. And we've got two P7s and next year when I'm in P7, I'm going be in the other P7.'

'Ah,' said Alex, 'that worked out well. So then, we'll see you Tuesday, and thank you so much for taking on Denzil . . . '

She grasped my hand again, this time it was a less successful handshake, she actually got one of her rings caught on a bit of rough nail I hadn't filed down. We both apologised awkwardly. Then Denzil obviously felt he ought to do the same thing, and he squeezed my fingers so tightly that I yelped, and we all laughed. Roisin looked daggers at his retreating back.

'Actually I've got Zoe coming round after school on Tuesday.'

'Well, you guys can stay in the garden. I won't be tutoring him in the garden, will I?'

'God forbid,' she said, comically, self-mockingly, and it gave me a little twinge because that's the way her dad always used to say it.

So on Tuesday, with Denzil looking longingly out into the back garden where Roisin and her friend Zoe were swinging in the apple tree, I dragged the kitchen table over to the small bay window in the living room area, that looked out into the street. The view of a sleepy row of houses couldn't be that much more exciting than eleven-plus questions, surely?

Well, it was a close-run thing. I'd been told he liked making things – dens and bivouacs and tents – so I thought we'd start off with some geometry. He could understand all those parallel lines and adjacent angles and opposite angles reasonably well, when they were on a diagram of a tent. But after twenty minutes he gave a deep sigh, obviously hoping the hour was nearly over, and pointed out a dog scratching itself on the fence across the road. So I produced a few ad hoc mathematical problems about dogs and fences, and he struggled mightily to concentrate, and afterwards we were both exhausted.

And Roisin asked, 'Why are you doing this?'

And I said, 'Roisin, you want to go and see your cousins in Canada this summer, don't you?'

'I thought you said it was cheap because I'm still under twelve?'

'No, mo chara, not cheap. Cheap*er*. We're still looking at six hundred pounds for me and three hundred pounds for you, plus we need to pay our way when we're out there, we can't rely on Uncle Geoff and Auntie Cath for everything, we'll need some spending money. So I want to raise fifteen hundred pounds by August, OK? And if I have two sessions a week with Denzil Masterton and two with Johnny McAfee, that should just about cover it . . . '

'So you won't be doing any more tutoring after August?'

'I wish. But I can't just dump them. I've got to see them through the eleven-plus, then after November there won't be any more tutoring.'

'Promise?'

'I promise.'

On Saturday, Denzil and I did prime numbers, square numbers, converting fractions to percentages and – our greatest achievement so far – how much does a £75 tent cost if it's reduced by twenty per cent? Of course he'd done all these things before. At his prep school. But his head just couldn't keep all that information in. By the time we'd worked out that the tent was an absolute snip at £60, he'd completely forgotten which were prime numbers and which were square numbers.

He gazed despondently round the room.

'Mrs Corcoran?'

'Yes?'

'Why d'you have pillars in your kitchen?'

'Well, you see, it was two tiny rooms, the kitchen and the living room, so we knocked down the dividing wall to make it into one big room. But we needed to put in the pillars, to make sure the ceiling didn't fall down!'

'Oh.' He grinned. 'Why is your house so small, when your garden's so big?'

'Well, after the First World War, when the soldiers came back, they didn't want to have to live in slums. So they got new houses, but they weren't very big because the soldiers were quite poor. It was all countryside 'round here then, way outside Belfast and there was lots of space, so they gave them big gardens to grow food for their families: carrots and potatoes and currant bushes.'

'When a soldier came back from the war, could he keep his horse in the garden?'

'Horse?'

'You know, like in *War Horse*, we went to see it in London last year.'

'Um, no. I think he had to give the horse back.'

'Oh. Why were the soldiers so poor?'

Before I knew it, we were in a discussion about class structure in Edwardian Ireland, and for someone who wasn't yet ten, he was asking quite intelligent questions. I thought of Johnny McAfee, and Roisin and her wee friends: it would never have occurred to any of them to ask why the house was so small, and the garden so big. Trouble was, asking intelligent questions wasn't going to help him pass the eleven-plus.

'OK,' I said, 'back to square numbers?'

He sighed. 'Back to square numbers.'

The sun poured down that week. The garden lost its spiky, bare, wintry look and became a place of fluttery green promise. All the buds were popping open on the bushes and next door's cherry blossom was drifting across on to our grass, and we could hear the *tsee tsee tsee* of blue tits. I wondered if they were nesting somewhere. Roisin played outside a lot, sometimes with a couple of girls from school or from up the street, pointedly ignoring Denzil on Tuesday and Johnny McAfee on Wednesday and Thursday and Denzil again on Saturday. On the Sunday, I got a rather peculiar phone call from Denzil's father.

'Mrs Corcoran?'

'Yes?'

'How much experience do you have?'

He had the brisk, slightly pompous tones of a headmaster. I hadn't asked Alex Masterton what her husband did, but he certainly sounded like he was used to having a lot of people answerable to him. I told him I'd been teaching P6 and P7 for eighteen years, and also taken little withdrawal groups for 'extra support' in maths, until the Board, in its infinite wisdom, decided to withdraw the funding for that particular post, because our kids weren't deprived enough.

'Ah. Well. I was wondering. Because I see you're only charging £25 an hour?'

'Did you expect me to be charging more?'

'One of my colleagues, whom I was speaking to yesterday, is paying £35 an hour for his daughter to be tutored.' It's not often you can hear the commas so clearly when someone's talking to you on the phone.

'So you think I mightn't be as good as this other tutor?'

A little dry, disclaiming cough.

'By no means. It has no implication for yourself. It's just that we had my son at a tutoring agency, which was naturally a bit cheaper, not being a one-to-one situation. He didn't do very well, and I felt afterwards that it was a false economy; he wasn't getting enough personal attention.'

'So if you pay more for something, it must be better?'

'Well, one would presume so.'

What a pompous git, I thought. I told him I was going to give Denzil a hundred and one percent personal attention, but if he thought Denzil would do better with a more expensive tutor, he should get one soon, because kids get unsettled if they're constantly getting different adults with different expectations lecturing them, and if he waited till next term and then changed Denzil's tutor, just before the exam, it might throw the lad off completely. He said he had no intention of making last-minute changes, and since I had an excellent reference from Mrs McAfee, and this other tutor of his colleague's daughter had only ten years' experience to my eighteen, he'd be quite happy to continue with my good self.

He sounded like such a dry old stick to be married to the colourful, jangly Alex. Next Tuesday she arrived late and, when Denzil's yawning hour was up, I ushered him out to wait in the garden. For once, Roisin had no other wee girls on the premises.

She and Denzil eyed each other suspiciously. Two girls, I thought, even if they didn't instantly make friends, they'd at least go on the swings and chat. But a girl of nearly eleven, with highly developed verbal skills, and a wee boy not even ten yet, who just wanted to climb and run about – what could they possibly have in common?

I poked at the lawn with the toe of my shoe. It was dry as a bone.

'Roisin,' I called, 'do you want to get the trampoline out?'

Denzil snapped suddenly awake.

'Yay! A trampoline!'

It wasn't that simple, the wretched thing was tucked away in its cover still slightly slimy from the winter and spring rains, under a pile of junk in the so-called car port. The three of us were still struggling to manhandle it out on to the lawn when Alex arrived. Denzil moaned, 'But we can't go yet, I haven't had a go yet', at which he and Roisin both laughed, and I could see the ice thawing, if not breaking.

Once it was up, Roisin started bouncing in her usual competent fashion; she'd been to a summer trampolining course the year before, and she could do knee drops, seat drops and twisting seat drops. Denzil tried a seat drop and couldn't get up again, so he started clowning around, pretending to be stuck, then pretending he was about to fall off, then he actually jumped off and landed like a cat, did a somersault and scrambled back up again. Alex's face softened as she watched him.

'Have you time for a coffee?' I asked.

'Oh yes,' she said, caught off guard, 'I always have time in the afternoons, the house is immaculate, I'm immaculate, what more is there to do? Except help Denzil with his homework, of course, and he'd take any excuse to put that off, and so would I.'

We stayed in the kitchen, in spite of the sunshine outside. She made me nervous, scanning the room, appraising the mess, as if she were looking for something which she was quite sure she wouldn't find. But I didn't want to be out in the garden, making Denzil and Roisin self-conscious.

I told her about the phone call. Her face went all pink.

'What? He rang you? He actually rang you?'

'Yeah, it was a bit disconcerting.'

'The nerve. The cheek of it. As if I couldn't have asked you myself. Does he not even trust me to organise tutoring for my own kid? Ha. Men. I hope he didn't leave you feeling undermined.'

'No. It's OK.'

'Well, he leaves me feeling hopelessly undermined. Honestly. He never helps Denzil with his homework, he's hardly ever back before eight and by that time Denzil's well and truly had it, he leaves it all for me to do and then he criticises—'

She gave a little snort and dropped two sugar lumps in her coffee. Instantly she fished them out again with a teaspoon and dumped them on the tray, where they sat in a leaky huddle, their whiteness tinged the apologetic pale brown colour of coffee icing. She sighed. 'Well, at least Denzil enjoys coming here.'

She didn't want me to comment on the husband. Besides, what could I possibly say that would be helpful? I heard myself gushing about Denzil and the trampoline, how it was great for kids to have some physical activity, it really helped their brains work, maybe I should give him five minutes on the trampoline next time before he started, I'd always loved trampolining myself, did she have a trampoline when she was a kid? And she positively flinched, as if I'd said something hostile. Looked at me with eyes as hard as pebbles, and said 'No, I didn't get a trampoline.' *Get*? As opposed to *have*?

She stood up, drained her cup, walked to the back door, gazed at the jumble of boxes and old bicycles and a rusty scooter and cracked plant pots. 'Where on earth do you keep your car?'

I said I didn't have one.

'Well! I don't know if that's a blessing or a disadvantage. The latter, I should think.' For a moment, she sounded just like the husband.

'Not really, we don't miss it,' I said, bending the truth a fair bit.

'Denzil!' she shouted. 'Time to go!' She turned back to me. 'Oh I couldn't possibly manage without a car of my own, the shopping, nipping out to the gym and the hairdresser, taking Denzil to his friends' houses and picking him up . . . '

'Well, Roisin's friends seem to come here, mostly.'

'Really?' She raised an ironic eyebrow in the direction of the pile of junk in the car port.

'Denzil!' she shouted again.

'Did you hear me? Get your shoes on!'

He scrambled down off the trampoline, and she chivvied him ahead of her into the kitchen. In the middle of the floor was a box labelled 'Locally Organic'; he bumped into it and sent onions rolling into every corner of the room. 'Denzil!' she scolded. 'Pick those up!'

'Well, it wasn't there before,' he complained.

'Sorry,' I said. 'I'd forgotten it was the veg man's day.'

He appeared at the front door, a scruffy, apologetic figure in a torn denim shirt, with another box in his arms, carrots and bananas heaped up in it.

'It's not my day, Mrs Corcoran, only I can't come tomorrow—'

At the sight of him, Alex stopped dead. She pulled Denzil towards her, away from the boxes, with exaggerated care, and brushed a bit of imaginary earth from his sweatshirt. She was positively glaring at the man. I could see how he must appear to her: a dusty, shabby offshoot of my unkempt, throughother house and garden.

'Well, we're off now,' she snapped. 'And that stuff may be organic, but in what sense could a banana be called locally grown produce?'

She was sounding like the husband again. She swept Denzil away without waiting for an answer. The veg man started unpacking the boxes. He would never sit down for a cup of coffee, but as long as he could stay on his feet, he was always happy to chat.

'People want fruit,' he explained, 'and I don't see many apples and pears on the trees at this time of year. That woman, honestly, everything has to be so perfect for her.'

'Oh, you know her?'

'Yes, I deliver for her too. She lives way up the Malone Road, right at the posh end, down a little posh lane . . . '

He started telling me about Alex Masterton, describing with a sort of appalled fascination her shiny metallic kitchen, huge glittering conservatory with its fingerprintless glass coffee tables, carefully arranged piles of glossy magazines featuring perfect social occasions and perfect interiors, some of which she was even in herself, not a hair out of place, and of course her pristine garden, not a weed in sight.

'And you know what I saw this morning? Cheeky fat bullfinches eating her cherry blossom. Well, they're in imminent danger of being shot,either by her or by that husband, who's even more OCD than she is. So she says.'

'What's a bullfinch?' Roisin was taking off her muddy trainers in the doorway.

'It's a big fat finch with a grey back and a pink front and a black cap. They're real good lookers, but the gardeners hate them because they eat all the blossom, and then the fruit can't grow.'

'Do you get cowfinches?' she asked.

'Yup. Cowfinches are a sort of brownish grey, and they eat just as much blossom, but nobody notices because they're so unobtrusive.'

'What's unobtrusive?'

'It means you blend in, nobody really notices you. It can be useful, especially if you're a bird.'

'So why are magpies black and white? And seagulls white? Because they're the kind of birds you really, really notice.'

He picked up his boxes, ready to go.

'Maybe one day you'll be a biologist and find out.'

Maybe it was Denzil who would one day be a biologist? As we ploughed our way through the turgid trails of exam papers, he seemed to wake up a bit whenever we came to a poem, because the poems were often about nature: birds, animals, pets, fish, farms, forests, the sea . . . if there was a word he couldn't read, he'd work away at it. He'd expect it to make sense for him, and eventually it would. Faced with 'Circle the best word to complete the sentence,' he'd mutter to himself, 'Fish that are sleeping, no, floating, no, darting, *yes*!' and triumphantly circle 'darting'. But faced with 'Tick the correct box in the table below to show which of these four words is used as an adjective, a verb, a noun or an adverb,' he'd practically dozed off before he'd finished reading the question. 'What's it *matter* if it's a verb or an adverb?' he'd ask plaintively. Once, asked to put five words in alphabetical order, he came up with: swimming, sleeping, startled, spluttering, saved. He furnished me with a perfectly logical explanation: if you're swimming in the sea, and you fall asleep, and someone startles you, then you start spluttering and you wake up and don't drown, so you're saved.

'But it's not in alphabetical order, Denzil!'

'Oh,' he said, sadly. 'I forgot.'

Disruptive? No, he was never disruptive. But after an initial burst of enthusiasm, perked up perhaps by the knowledge that I wasn't going to shout at him or embarrass him in front of other kids, he rapidly slumped again. He would yawn and gaze out of the window dreamily, as if his dreams were much more interesting than anything on the test paper. They probably were. After a couple more sessions, I decided to row back a bit and concentrate on one topic at a time, instead of ploughing chronologically through a whole paper. He got so confused, one minute being asked to 'calculate the difference between the maximum and minimum temperatures for Saturday and Sunday' then, just when he'd got the hang of that, being asked to find the cost of 120 centimetres of ribbon, then being asked to answer questions on what looked like the beginning of a ghost story, then just when it was getting interesting, it was back to maths again and how much did Mary pay for a dress if it was reduced by twenty percent?

'Why does it keep jumping about from one thing to another?' he'd complain.

Jumping about from one thing to another was

probably just what he'd been told not to do, by a succession of teachers from about P2 onwards. So I said alright, we'd do half an hour of maths and then half an hour of English, but he said it would be better to do the English first, because it wasn't as bad as the maths. At this point Roisin chimed in that of course, if you have maths homework and English homework, you *always* do English first, because it's more fun. Denzil looked astonished at the idea that any aspect of homework could ever be seen as fun.

I cast my mind back, way back. When did I reach the age where I stopped doing the fun things first, and started doing 'nasties' first, to get them out of the way? Was it when I got to grammar school? Or maybe not till I had marking and lesson plans and an infant Roisin as well? Was that when I finally reached maturity and learned to prioritise? I asked Denzil's mum when she came to pick him up, car engine still running and her tut-tutting as to how long he was taking to get his stuff together. She was obviously a well-organised woman. Could she remember what she was like at that age, nine going on ten? Did she still want to do the fun things first and put off the nasties as long as possible?

There it was again. That hard, closed-down look.

'No,' she said, 'I really can't remember that much about primary school. Denzil, come *on*.'

I could feel a miasma of uneasiness, almost

hostility, hanging in the air. Even Denzil was catching it, he picked up his schoolbag upside down and open, and everything fell out and he had to start again. Outside in the garden, I could hear the soft thud of Roisin kicking a ball against the wall, and, in the pauses, the triumphant, sunshiny trill of a chaffinch. I asked Mrs Masterton, would she not have time for a cup of coffee?

'Oh no,' she said, 'he has tennis at twelve o'clock.'

'Tennis?'

'That's right. He doesn't want to go to the junior rugby on Saturday mornings, so my husband said OK, provided he took up another sport not karate or something, a proper sport that he could carry on with at grammar school. So we settled on tennis.'

That was the day I started thinking, *What the hell have I taken on here?* He was a bright enough kid, he was very articulate, but we only had six months to bring him up to eleven-plus level. He just wouldn't be ready. In a year's time, maybe. And I didn't relish the prospect of discussing this with his mother. She could pass, in an instant, from bright and jolly, ruffling his hair and being tolerant about his total off-the-ball-ness, to uptight, tense, almost fierce. Looking at me as if I was a disorganised, cobwebs-in-the-kitchen, no-car-in-the-nonexistent-garage failure, and as if my failure would rub off on Denzil. No, I thought, I'll stagger on for another couple of weeks before I start this discussion.

But on Tuesday she was beaming.

'Yes, before you ask, I do have time for a cup of coffee!'

She had the kettle on before I could clear up the eleven-plus papers. Then she produced a bag of massive chocolatey tray bakes and told Roisin and Denzil to take them into the garden and demolish the lot. After grabbing a couple back, she settled onto my sofa – actually tucked her feet up under her – and then said, 'Well! I've got a job!'

'Oh, I never asked you what you do?'

'Well, I used to be a nurse, and I gave it up when Stewart and Chloe were little and somehow I never had the strength to go back to it, I just swanned about the place getting my hair done and going to the gym and having manicures and pedicures and generally being a sort of trophy wife. Honestly, you've no idea how much energy that takes.'

'So what are you doing now?'

'I'm in a café, believe it or not. I'm a sort of glorified sandwich and panini maker, drinks server and table wiper. It's a very cool place, it's called Lunch at Louisa's, a friend of mine runs it and she's so fed up with all these dopey girls who ignore the customers and talk about their boyfriends, the other day she said she wanted somebody more mature. She was absolutely delighted when I said I was free from eleven to three every day.'

She gushed on and on, while I sat there feeling

unjustifiably sour. So she was going to earn some pin money, and probably spend the lot on make-up and glossy magazines, what else could she possibly need in that swish *Ulster Tatler* house of hers? Meanwhile, I would carry on struggling into school at half eight every morning, braced for the arrival of kids who were getting more and more fidgety as the Easter holidays approached. Only one more week of term, and they couldn't wait, they were like wild birds; they'd swoop down and imbibe a little sensible good-for-your-brain nourishment, but you couldn't keep them on the bird table, they were itching to fly away.

Sometimes I felt like I was the bird table, sort of damp and flat and trampled on by hundreds of tiny, scratchy feet. I'd crawl home every day, and when I'd finished my endless round of marking and writing up and box ticking, and when Roisin had told me all her troubles and I'd conquered the overwhelming urge to tell her mine, I'd just collapse in front of the TV or on a damp plastic chair on my overgrown terrace, trying not to think of all the things I should be doing, like making more of an effort with Roisin, taking her to the library and getting her more proper books – surely it was time she moved on from Jacqueline Wilson – like being more patient, more organised, applying for more promoted posts, how if I was serious about my career I really ought to be a VP by now. I realised I was folding an eleven-plus paper, ridiculously, incongruously into the shape of a sailing boat, smoothing its crisp edges.

And she said, 'I do worry about him, you know. I've got to do something to take my mind off things.'

We looked at each other and I thought, *Is this the moment when I'm going to say, 'Mrs Masterton I don't think this is going to work out with Denzil, I'm starting to feel like I'm taking your money under false pretences.'*

Then I heard Roisin shout, 'Mum! Come and see what we're doing!'

Out in the garden, they were making a den. They'd dragged branches off the old rowan tree, quite thick ones clustered with dense ivy, and propped them up in the gaunt rhododendron bush beside the terrace, so it looked like a sort of camouflaged Army bivouac. I could just see Denzil's face poking out. Roisin, looking slightly defiant, was standing a couple of paces back from the structure, so she could distance herself from the whole thing if I showed signs of disapproval. A couple of wood pigeons were sitting up in one of the apple trees, looking indignant. They liked to eat the ivy berries; they'd been put out of their usual stamping ground.

'What is it?' I shouted down the garden.

'It's a tent! We're playing camping!'

Denzil's Mum turned to me.

'I'm so sorry, I had no idea he'd start destroying your garden.'

'No, really, it's fine,' I said. 'There's not much garden here to destroy, it's half-ruined already.'

Roisin, seeing I hadn't come down the garden to stop them, had started to lug stones out of the overgrown flower bed and place them in a circle in front of the shaggy green tent. I could see what she was doing: making a place for a camp fire. Denzil was snapping sticks into short lengths and expertly propping them up together in a quite convincing wigwam shape that looked as if it might actually light, if I was fool enough to give them some matches.

'That's exactly what I used to do,' I marvelled. I started rambling on about how I used to play at camping with my best friend, and we had an old sheet draped over the lowest branch of the apple tree in my garden, but we were going to save up all our birthday moneys and the money we got for passing the eleven-plus, and buy a real tent and go camping in the Mournes. Sadly it all went pear-shaped after the eleven-plus results came out, but in any case we would never have been let, we wouldn't even have been let go camping in the local park, two ten year olds, can you imagine?'

'No,' said Denzil's Mum coldly, 'I can't imagine. Imagination has never been my strong point.'

She was gazing down the garden, not at Roisin and Denzil, but at the apple tree with its empty swing.

Then she said, 'Excuse me,' and turned and went back into the house.

I started picking up a couple of tray bake wrappers that had landed on the lawn, but right away she was back, with her big glossy turquoise handbag, riffling about in it, and was so clumsy that she actually managed to drop it, so a cascade of lipsticks and keys and tissues and a purse – white, of all colours – ended up in the muddy grass. Roisin came over and tried to be helpful, picking up her bits and pieces, but she snapped 'Leave it!' Roisin went a bit pink and backed off, causing the woman to apologise, but stiffly and awkwardly. She was holding her mobile – the one thing that hadn't fallen.

She said, 'I was just checking my dates. Yes, we're going on the third of April, that's actually next Monday, so Denzil has one more session before that, and I'd be grateful if you could let him have a couple of practice papers for while we're away.'

'Away?'

'Skiing. Andorra. For a week. All five of us. I presume it won't hurt him to miss a week? It's only two sessions.'

'Of course not.'

'Oh, and next Saturday, it's important that he comes out quickly, so could you just send him out bang on eleven and I'll wait in the car?'

'Of course.'

And she swept up the contents of her handbag,

and Denzil, in what seemed like one fierce, efficient gesture, and headed for the car, and I wondered what was eating the woman, because obviously it couldn't be anything to do with what I'd been saying?

And Roisin wanted to know could we not go skiing some time, and I got a bit snappy too, thinking of all the expense of Canada in the summer, then I had to apologise, so that was two apologies she'd received in one day. Pretty unusual.

She went indoors and switched the TV on, and I sank down into one the garden chairs, damp as it was, nibbled in a half-hearted way at the one remaining tray bake and gazed up at the sky. There was a sort of ribbed effect, like when you're walking on the beach and the tide's gone out and the sand sort of bulges and glimmers. I could hear what sounded like oystercatchers flying over, though it was probably just the starlings in the trees all around, doing those surprising sea bird imitations they sometimes do. I thought of the sea, and Canada, and the vast Ontario lakes, and Geoff and Cath's cabin, and barbecues on the beach.

I tried not to think about how much our grass needed cutting. How the hedge was all straggly, from never being properly trimmed last autumn. How the weeds were already poking up between the cracked paving stones of the terrace. I thought of Alex Masterton's pristine garden, as described by the veg man: not much danger of me ever being invited to see it, to be overwhelmed by its glossy under-control-ness, and the intimidating glitter of her giant conservatory.

A magpie was strutting across the trampoline and I went over to put the cover on, but it was too late, there was a big sticky gob of bird shit across the mesh. I poked at it with a twig. 'I never got a trampoline', Alex had said, and it seemed so incongruous; she came across as a woman who'd always had everything she wanted.

Catch yourself on, I told myself. Will you for dearsakes stop thinking about her? It's nearly Easter. Just one more session with all-over-the-place Denzil, and his twitchy unpredictable mother, then you're going to get ten days off.

Peace, perfect peace. Without either of them. Be thankful. It'll be great, I told myself.

Honestly. It will. Just great.

APRIL

Of course, things are never what you hope for. I didn't have Denzil, staring out of the window and sighing, but I had a surprising amount of bother with Roisin. Her dad and his new family were off to Donegal for a week, and he, dear bless him, not only did he turn her down when she rather pathetically asked to come along, which was fair enough because it was only a two-bedroom cottage, but he actually forgot to mention that they were leaving on the second of April, which was a Sunday, so Roisin was waiting for him to come and pick her up. She usually spent Sundays at his house, but nobody came for her.

I asked her if she wanted to go to the cinema, but she said No, she just wanted to stay in and watch a DVD. Sunday is the one day in the week that I sometimes watch a daytime film. So I left Roisin being me, curled up on the sofa hugging the big cushions, but without the glass of Tesco's Finest Chianti. I went upstairs and switched on the computer and started trying to cobble together a worksheet about the vikings. My own pathetic excuses were ringing in my ears: Daddy doesn't mean to upset you, he's just got a very busy job and two small children and that's a lot of work, he just forgets.

Poor Rory. He never could organise a piss-up in a brewery. When Denise married him, she said she realised he was completely throughother, but it was part of his charm. I wonder if she still thinks that?

I was only trying to cut and paste, dear knows I should be able to do that, but the vikings were giving me a lot of bother. I ended up with a truncated picture of half a galley. The doorbell rang. I ignored it, managed to get the whole galley in, but half my text had got chopped off. It rang again, and I heard Roisin's voice raised in protest.

'For goodness sake! I'm trying to concentrate on my DVD! Why do I have to have the doorbell rung by a whole lot of stupid vegetables!'

I looked out the window and, right enough, there was the van, 'Locally Organic'. I trundled down the stairs.

'Oh come on, Roisin, it wouldn't have taken you two seconds to open the door.'

The veg man came in with a loaded box, brimming with apologies, he had to take the van to the garage on Monday so he was trying to pack three days' deliveries into Sunday, sorry for the disturbance, sorry for the rush. Roisin had paused the TV and was glaring at us. She didn't appreciate my exhortations to help unpack the box.

'Not carrots again,' she moaned. 'I hate carrots!'

'Roisin, get a grip. You sound like a four year old.'

'I wish I was a four year old! Then I'd be allowed to watch the Moomins in peace!'

She dumped the carrots on the kitchen table and took the stairs two at a time. I heard her bedroom door slam. Then it was my turn to be full of apologies, and he said honestly, not to worry, this was just the start of it, the door-slamming years, they have to get worse before they get better, don't they?

'Oh, do you have kids?'

He gave a little shrug.

'No kids so far. But a pretty good spread of nephews and nieces.'

He picked up the DVD box. 'Moomins, The Complete Series One? Three hundred and twenty-eight minutes? That should buy plenty of peace and quiet. After I've gone.'

'I used to read the book to her,' I said.

'There's a magic hat that a sort of jungle grows out of, just like our completely jungley wild garden, she always loved that bit. I didn't even know we had a DVD of it.'

And then I realised where she'd probably got it.

I must have looked so sad, he asked 'What's the matter?'

'I remember now, she told me she'd been watching it at Rory's house. My ex. With his kids. And they're away on holiday, and they didn't invite her . . . and she's sort of watching their leavings . . . that's a bit painful . . . '

He didn't say 'Oh well' or 'Never mind'. He just said, 'Yeah, everything's so intense at that age, I can just about remember. When you're ten. You think you're going to die because of the unfairness of it all.'

We looked at each other, and he picked up his two empty boxes and departed. Poor Roisin. It rained on and off for most of the week, and although she had plenty of friends over, they were pretty much cooped up in the house. She wanted to get them outside, rain and all, to play in the den and make an obstacle course, which she'd been planning to do with Denzil, but none of them seemed to feel up to braving the damp. They watched TV and fiddled with each other's hair and painted each other's nails, like they couldn't wait till they were teenagers.

'Why don't we have a car?' Roisin bleated.

'Well, it wouldn't stop the rain if we did.'

'But we could go swimming, you could take us to the Lisburn Leisureplex and me and my friends could go on the water slides!'

'We can anyway, *mo chara*, it's just we'd need to get two buses so it would take quite a lot longer.'

'Can we do it tomorrow?'

I explained that I had Johnny McAfee coming at two o'clock, incredibly inconvenient, and that we wouldn't be able to get to Lisburn and back in time unless we set off at the crack of dawn.

'Why is he coming at two o'clock?'

'Because he's got to go to the dentist in the morning. For a filling. There are people who have even more boring lives than you, Roisin.'

She gave me a sour look. She flounced off, and I could hear her banging a football off the back wall of the house. Thud. Pause. Thud. Pause. I sighed, and went back to marking Johnny McAfee's exam papers. He was barely averaging sixty per-cent. I bundled up the exam papers and took them outside with a couple of towels, one to dry the plas-tic table and one to stop my skirt getting soaked when I sat on a damp plastic chair. There was a puddle on the table, and a wood pigeon drinking out of it. It looked at me indignantly and flew away with a derisive clap of its wings. I tipped the puddle on to the grass, wiped the table, and started mark-ing. What did it matter if Johnny's test papers got a bit damp? Roisin came over and started reading over my shoulder.

'Wow,' she said, 'he doesn't even know fifty per-cent is a half. I thought everybody knew that. Even Denzil knows that.'

'He does know,' I said. 'He's just so on edge all the time, he gets confused and forgets.'

Roisin seldom gets confused. 'You know what?' she said. 'I'm not having any girls over on Tuesdays next term.'

'Really? Why not?'

'Well, it bothers Denzil. He can't play with girls, he feels stupid. And I don't want him to be on edge. Because then he won't be able to concentrate and then he won't do well in the tests.'

I asked as gently as I could, 'Would it really be so awful if he didn't do well?'

'Oh yeah, he said his dad would be livid if he didn't get a high mark.'

'Would he?'

'Yeah, his dad said if he couldn't get into a grammar school, he'd be stuck in some awful secondary school with teachers who can't keep order and kids who only want to leave school at sixteen and go on the dole. Mum?'

'Yes?'

'Do kids who go to the integrated school end up on the dole?'

'No,' I said, 'absolutely not. They all get good jobs, and some of them who work hard go to university, and then they get even better jobs.'

There didn't seem to be much point in telling her that I'd been on the dole myself a couple of times, before I got the job at Unity. Everything's so black and white at her age. And she wouldn't want to hear a long grey answer, about integrated schools being much better because you get Catholic and Protestant and middle class and working class and academic and non-academic, all in together, but yeah, there are still some apparently perfectly rational adults who think their kids are doomed if they don't go to grammar school – if I started explaining all this, she'd get bored in the middle and switch off, wouldn't she? She just wanted a black answer or a white answer, and I gave her a white answer, didn't I?

'Oh,' she said. 'Does that mean Denzil's dad's wrong?'

I looked her straight in the eye. 'Yeah, don't say I said this, but yeah, Denzil's dad's definitely wrong.'

So that was a black answer, and she appeared satisfied.

*

And then it was Tuesday, and the rain had stopped and the lawn dried up, and Denzil was due for another session, having been back from Andorra for two days, and didn't his Mum ring up just an hour before, saying he'd come home with a shocking cold and he'd been awake half the night coughing, he could barely keep his eyes open, and would it be better to put the session off? I told her of course, make it Friday, he should have had a chance to catch up on his sleep by then.

And Roisin wailed, 'But Claire and Zoe wanted to come over today and I told them not to, because Denzil was coming, and now they've gone to Pickie Park in Bangor instead and it's too late for me to go with them!'

Oh, misery. I sometimes think I'd be a better teacher, and maybe even a better mother, if I didn't remember so clearly what it's like to be utterly squashed and flattened by the miseries of childhood. Whatever about the veg man's opinion, my VP says there's such a thing as too much empathy, it can stop you being firm with them at times, when it's firmness that's really needed.

So when it started to rain and Roisin begged 'Can we do the boxes now I'm so bored can we do the boxes now pleasepleaseplease?'

I said 'Well, just one.'

And if I hadn't said that, maybe everything would have been different.

The boxes had emerged in January, when Roisin got a new bed with a storage drawer underneath to keep all those cuddlies and Barbies she was getting too old for, but couldn't bear to part with. Then, embarrassingly, it emerged that there were three boxes of mine squashed under her old bed: stuff I hadn't unpacked since I got my first job and moved into a flat, stuff that went back through to my student years. And teenage years. And right back into my childhood. I'd told her there was no way we were going to start unpacking all that old stuff at the start of the new term, I'd tucked the boxes into the spare room beside the computer and thrown a rug over them and said, if you're desperate to start noseying about, maybe at Easter.

'I want the one from when you were at primary school,' she said. 'Is there stuff from when you were my age?'

There was. There was a layer of Barbies, with clothes ranging from shop-bought and tacky to home-made and tacky. Roisin was amazed to hear that when I was ten I did sewing at school, while the boys did handwork, and that if you finished all your sewing ahead of the others, you were allowed to sew a skirt for one of your Barbie dolls. Then she unearthed my old Girls' Brigade uniform and pranced about with it on, the hat made her look like a cartoon character from the 1950s, a weird sort of pillbox thing with an elastic that went under your chin, so that it wouldn't fall off if you marched too vigorously.

'What did you do in the Girls' Brigade?'

'Well, we marched . . . and we collected money for the crippled children's outing . . . and we marched . . . and we sewed . . . and we marched.'

'And what's this, it looks like a birthday present, why's it still wrapped up?'

A small square box, smaller than I remembered, wrapped in bright orange paper, tied round with a shiny yellow ribbon in a squashed kind of bow. I spent ages learning how to do those bows back in the 1980s, before they'd invented special bags that cost £1.50 and said 'Happy Birthday'.

She was unwrapping it very carefully.

I said 'Don't—' but she'd already opened the box and lifted out the present, holding it up high, dangling the silvery chain from her fingers so that the little coloured glass pendant swung to and fro.

And it glittered. It must have been thirty years old but, safe in its box, it hadn't dulled or got scratched. In the sleepy gloom of the kitchen, it caught brightness from somewhere, sparkling and spinning round and round in her hands, flaring with light.

'What is it?' she asked, in awe.

'It's a swallow.'

It has dark blue arched wings and a forked tail, smart white underneath, and a wee red patch under its chin. It's the prettiest necklace I've ever seen, and it costs five weeks' pocket money. I just know I have to get Sandra something special, because during all those five long weeks she hasn't once spoken to me. But this will make everything alright.

It's Saturday, and I know today is her birthday, because I still have last year's party invitation sellotaped to my wardrobe door. I trail up her street, getting slower as I get near her house. I love this street: the houses are tiny, like gingerbread houses, red brick you could almost eat, and there are no front gardens, so everybody props their bikes and scooters and doll's prams up against their house wall. And everybody plays in the street. I wish I was allowed to play in the street.

I stand on her doorstep. Her mother looks at me uneasily.

'Is Sandra in?'

'Oh,' her mother says. 'Just a minute.' She looks back into the house and leaves me standing there. Why doesn't she say 'Come on in' like she usually does? There's a lot of noise coming from the kitchen. Loud music and shrieks of laughter. A sudden bang, like a gun firing. Or maybe a balloon popping.

Sandra's mother is back. 'She's at her Granny's,' she says 'I'll tell her you called.'

'Oh.' I'm struggling to believe her; I have to believe her, because I'm eleven and she's a grown-up.

'Could you give her this please?' I ask in my special talking-to-grown-ups voice.

She doesn't have a special voice for talking

to children. She just takes the box and says 'Oh, aye, I'll give it to her.' And then, with a certain amount of effort, 'Thank you very much.'

And closes the door rather quickly. I trail home, through Carson Street and Dufferin Street, across the main road and into my home world, where the streets are all called Crescent and Avenue and Gardens and you're not allowed to play in them, because of all the cars, even in the cul-de-sacs. You're supposed to play in the back gardens, and what use is that when your brother's out there playing football with his best friend and they don't want to play with a girl, and your best friend won't play with you because suddenly she's not your best friend any more?

In the morning, when we're all setting off for church and my dad opens the front door, he nearly trips over something that's been left on the step. There it is, the little box, its yellow paper all crumpled because it's obviously been unwrapped and re-wrapped, and the ribbon clumsily re-tied. I dash indoors with it, I bury it under my pillow. We're late already so my parents don't ask me about it, and they don't ask me why I'm sitting in church all snuffly, they just assume I'm getting a cold.

I don't want it back, why would I want it

back? I think about giving it to the teacher, she's making up a box for the orphans in Africa, full of sweets and little presents. For Easter. But when I think of it stuck in amongst the hair bobbles and felt tip pens and chocolate eggs, it just makes the whole thing seem even sadder. So I bury it deep in the bottom of a drawer, under my old GB uniform which I don't need any more; I'm giving up GB because there'll be lots of more important things to do, once I start at grammar school.

And seven years later, when I'm leaving for university, everything in the drawer gets stuffed into a big cardboard box. That box follows me around through my next few moves, unopened.

'Can I put it on?' Roisin asked me.

'Yeah, sure. I don't want it.'

'Why don't you want it?'

'Because, long ago, it was a present for my best friend, but she wouldn't take it and that was . . . mmm . . . a bit upsetting.'

'Why wouldn't she take it?'

'She wasn't speaking to me.'

'Why not? Did you have a fight?'

'Oh, Roisin, it was ages ago, could be thirty years ago, I can't really remember . . . I know she was cross with me, but I don't think it was my fault . . . '

Roisin stood there dangling the swallow, slanting it backwards and forwards so it caught the light.

She said, 'Are you not going to tell me?' in a sulky, defeated voice.

She was still craving those black and white answers, and all I could give her was an unsatisfactory grey answer, I could see no purpose at all in dragging up all that old stuff, I just took the wee necklace out of her hands and clasped it round her neck and told her to go and look at herself in the mirror, and then why didn't we make pancakes, seeing it was nearly supper-time?

'It's lovely,' she said, doubtfully. 'Can I keep it?' I said she was welcome, and all the time we were mixing the batter she kept fiddling with it, and when the first pancake was in the pan, she went over to the mirror to look at herself again. Actually the wee swallow was so blue, it didn't quite go with her brown eyes and brown hair. She frowned. 'It feels strange. It feels like I'm pretending to be your best friend. Can I take it off?'

I said of course she could, and obviously mothers and daughters couldn't be best friends, it would be downright creepy, and why didn't we give it to a charity shop?

'No,' she said firmly. 'We need to keep it.'

She found some sellotape – Roisin is good at finding things, better than me – and carefully wrapped it up again. Then she tied the orange ribbon round it, and put it in the kitchen drawer where I keep the table mats and the best table-cloth I never use.

'That's where it is,' she explained, 'in case you ever want it.'

'Well, I wouldn't want it, not now.'

She asked me, what if I met my best friend again? I said if I met my best friend thirty years later, I probably wouldn't even recognise her, and what will we have with the pancakes, fried onions and cheese or bananas and chocolate?

But afterwards, when she'd gone upstairs to switch on the computer and look at endless photos of her Uncle Geoff's lakeside cottage in Canada and his kids waterskiing and wakeboarding and larking about and splashing each other, I went out into the garden and sat on one of the swings that hung from the big apple tree. The rain had stopped. It was almost dark, but the blackbirds were still singing their rich, velvety songs: disturbing somehow, as if in the grip of some obscure emotion, which you, the listener, had to work out. I kicked my feet into the wet grass to get the swing going.

It made me feel slightly queasy – too many pancakes, perhaps, or too many half-digested emotions that shouldn't be stirred up. I remembered this feeling from my childhood; the more you swing, the queasier you feel, but all the same, it's better than sitting still.

*

And then it was Friday, and they were back. Scruffy Denzil and his glossy mother. At half past three, after she'd finished at her friend's café. Both of them slightly sun-tanned, or wind-tanned, perhaps. And she'd brought me something from the Duty Free at the airport. A bottle of some liqueur thing with almost fluorescent lemons fizzing off the label.

'Och,' I said, 'you shouldn't have.'

Because I really, really would have preferred it if she hadn't.

'It's Limoncello,' she said, 'they were two for one. It's really refreshing on ice, it's for those hot summer days we're going to have, ha! No, seriously, it's awfully good of you to put up with Denzil.'

I made some deprecating sort of remark and Denzil rolled his eyes. She ruffled his hair and departed, leaving a trail of perfume in the air – also from the Duty Free, presumably. I recognised it: 'La Vie est Belle.' Shop assistants had been puffing it at me every time I went into the big chemist, it was being promoted everywhere, with pictures of that actress and her huge, implausible smile.

'So how was your holiday?' I asked Denzil.

'Really great,' he enthused, telling me how they'd skied down all the blue runs but only he and his brother and his dad had skied down the red runs, and only his dad had skied down the black runs. His dad said he was coming on a treat, and they didn't want to lose him in a fatal accident just yet.

'And I revised all my fractions and decimals and percentages with my dad,' he said proudly.

So we spent a peaceful half hour on fractions and decimals and percentages, working out equivalents and putting things in order of size. He concentrated fervently. Then we spent half an hour picking out mistakes in a couple of imaginary brochures. I'd even asked Roisin, when she was at the boredom stage, to type an article from the free newspaper for me, and put in some mistakes.

'When does Roisin have her coaching?' he asked.

I told him Roisin wasn't having any coaching. His eyes opened up like saucers, like the dog in the Grimms' fairy tale.

'Nearly everyone in my class is having coaching,' he said. 'Roisin must be awfully smart.'

'Well, she isn't doing the tests.'

'But I thought you had to!'

'No. Only if you want to go to a grammar school. Roisin's going to the integrated school.'

There was a long, long pause. I'd never known Denzil to be so quiet for so long. Then,

'Could I go to the integrated school?'

I heard myself umming and erring and faffing about, completely unconvincingly, saying it wouldn't work, it wouldn't be possible, it wasn't what his mum and dad wanted, and obviously it was up to them . . .

'Oh.'

Christ, I thought, *I've completely undermined the whole enterprise, I should have seen that coming.* But maybe it was just as well. He was going to tell his parents and they were going to think, 'What on earth are we doing having our son coached by a woman whose own daughter isn't even doing the eleven-plus? Isn't it bound to put him off trying?' And the whole arrangement would be off, and perhaps it would be just as well, because I wasn't sure I could survive till next November, coaching two wee boys, both of whom were probably going to fail.

Roisin was standing in the doorway, looking uncharacteristically shy, but determined. 'So what about this obstacle course then?'

It had started to rain again, just a light mist of rain, like being inside a cloud. But it didn't seem to bother either of them. When Denzil's mum came back, they were busy tying an old bit of trellis to the swings, so that you could edge along it from one swing to the other, swaying wildly. Apparently it was no longer an obstacle course, at least not in any competitive sense, but a sort of high ropes course, for getting right round the garden without touching the ground. I asked had she time for a coffee, and she said there was no hurry, neither of them had to be anywhere.

'You know, um, maybe we should talk about, um, how things are going . . . '

'Oh, put it off for another couple of weeks,' she said. 'We're all still glowing from our holiday. Wait till term gets going again and reality starts to kick in.'

She drank the coffee and chatted brightly about après-ski, and Lunch at Louisa's. Whatever was eating her just before Easter seemed to have disappeared. There'd been some quality time with Derek, and he'd conceded that Denzil was giving the eleven-plus his best shot, and what with the Cubs and the football, he could give up the tennis for the time being. Chloe was giving things up too, she had her A levels in just six weeks, it seemed a good time to slim down commitments. 'Denzil doesn't really enjoy the tennis,' his Mum commented. 'There's just no prospect of getting muddy.'

Roisin and Denzil had found an old plastic bin in the undergrowth, and it now formed part of their challenge course. It lay on its side and they had to edge along it, as it rolled in the slippery grass, then grab a rope and swing up into the rhododendron bush. Denzil's mum said, as they seemed to be getting on so well, was there any chance she could leave him for an extra hour after the Saturday session, and pick him up at lunchtime? I said of course, I even found myself asking would they like to stay at lunchtime and have a sandwich with us, but her face closed down again and she said no, Derek was coming home from the golf course especially early so they could have a family lunch, and having set this up, she couldn't very well wriggle out of it.

On Saturday Denzil was bright-eyed and bushy-tailed. The last trace of his cold seemed to be gone.

He asked, 'Was I trying very hard today?'

'Yes, Denzil, you were trying very hard.'

'Because my dad said, I really have to do this. He said I don't want to end up going to Rushfield like my mum.'

Rushfield. Home of the Millies with the chewing gum and the spray tans and the bleached blonde hair with roots showing. And the wee hard lads who drank vodka behind the outside toilets and sprayed UVF on the walls. And were probably in the UVF too. Rushfield. When I was eleven-plus age, that was where all the messers and no-hopers went, pretending they didn't care anyway, who'd want to go to grammar school with all those stuck-up kids and all that homework? And my best friend. That's where she went. I'll never forget the flat, dead sound of her voice when I rang her up, and said, 'Sandra, I got an A!' My mum says I can go to any school I want! And I'm getting a trampoline for passing the eleven-plus! And she said, 'Well I got a C,' and I kept saying 'No you couldn't have, you couldn't have got a C,' and then the line went dead.

I stared at Denzil and took a deep breath. I couldn't have heard him right.

'You don't mean Rushfield, Denzil, was it Rathmore?'

'No, it was Rushfield, he said she only got a C, she couldn't get into any of the grammar schools. And she didn't like Rushfield. So I have to try really hard not to go there. Am I only going to get a C?'

'The grades are different nowadays, it's not As and Bs and Cs any more. It's a numerical score. And we don't know what you're going to get. November is a long way off, now go on out and play.' He must have seen something in my face that he wasn't accustomed to seeing, because he didn't say one more word. He just slunk out into the garden.

I looked at his mum, when she came to pick him up. Today she was wearing a blue linen two-piece: a top with pockets and cropped drawstring trousers, casual but tasteful, definitely very expensive. Her hair was still that careful blonde, with a few silvery and coppery highlights, plausible enough for a woman who must be nearly the same age as me, and certainly no roots showing. They wouldn't dare. Women like her never went to Rushfield. They went to grammar schools, where there weren't any Millies. She must have worked pretty hard, to forget Rushfield. She must have really struggled to reinvent herself.

She snapped at Denzil to hurry up, because Chloe already had the lunch on, and when he asked 'Is dad coming?' she said, 'No, he has to work.'

To me she added, 'Apparently I got the day wrong, he said Sunday, and he couldn't imagine how I'd got mixed up with Saturday, don't I know he always works on Saturdays? Didn't take long for all that attentive father stuff to wear off. So we could have stayed here with you, only now we can't, because I already asked Stewart and Chloe to make one hundred percent sure they'd be there.'

For the first time, I found myself standing in the doorway, watching as she fussed Denzil into the car and drove away.

She'd got a new car; that hadn't been mentioned. It was a Peugeot, but painted up like the Minis they have nowadays, with two broad stripes down its nose, black on bright green. Really unusual. Not exactly a trophy-wife car, but not the sort of car you'd normally see round here, either. The street looked dull and empty when it had gone.

On Sunday Roisin went to her dad's as usual, and I sat outside at the plastic table with a huge pile of marking. Over my head, a rope ladder stretched from the rhododendron bush right across to the small apple tree, where it was securely knotted around the trunk. If you had strong wrists, you could swing across the round wooden rungs as if they were monkey bars in a playground. Where on earth had they got the rope ladder? Did Denzil bring it?

It was crisp and a bit chilly, but the sun was out. Collared doves were murmuring in the apple trees, a sleepy kind of sound. I could smell someone's Sunday roast, and hear their radio, distantly. I finished the last maths jotter, and riffled, bored, through yesterday's *Belfast Telegraph*. And there she was again, Alex Masterton, in a group photo: a bunch of beaming girls in cool outfits at a charity fashion show.

Fortyish 'girls', that is, glamorous and well-groomed, not a hair out of place, nothing brash. I could just imagine the schools they went to. Methody, Victoria College, Friends School Lisburn. But not Rushfield. Surely. She was like a cuckoo in the nest. I folded up the paper, annoyed with myself. It was all years ago. What did it matter what school she'd been to? I hefted a big pile of English jotters onto the plastic table and got started on them, trying not to dwell on the fact that it obviously mattered a lot to Derek Masterton, to his wife and now, apparently, to Denzil.

Someone was shouting in the distance.

'Hello? Excuse me? hello?'

I realised, with a start, that it was me he was shouting at. It was the veg man, standing at the side of the house, beside the pile of junk in the car port, sort of leaning round into the garden, and looking incredibly embarrassed.

'I'm so sorry, I didn't mean to startle you, I rang the bell, but nobody answered, I'm really sorry to bother you, I just came to apologise.'

'What? For startling me?'

His face relaxed into a grin.

'No. For giving your daughter a rope ladder. No, honestly, don't get up—'

He was striding up the lawn as I settled back into my chair. He gestured at the contraption above my head.

'I realised afterwards, it must seem like a weird thing to do. Only she saw it in the back of my van, I was taking some old stuff to the dump, she said could she and the young fella have it for their high ropes course? I couldn't think of any reason why not. I mean, it was only going to be thrown away. Then afterwards I thought, what if she falls off it, or she strangles herself in it, like that unfortunate wee kid that was in the paper recently, who strangled himself on the cord of a blind?'

'That kid was only three. Roisin's nearly eleven. I don't mind you giving her a rope ladder.'

He grinned again. 'Right. And you don't mind about all this then?'

I shook my head. We contemplated the scruffy garden, now with the added interest of bits of rope, bits of trellis and a muddy bin lying on its side.

'My garden wasn't exactly well-groomed to start with. But I was wondering, why did you have an old rope ladder, anyway?'

It was in his mother's shed, he explained. He went to see his mother every week, and she had loads of old stuff that had been there twenty, thirty years; that old rope ladder was made by his dad, to get him and his brothers up into the tree house, also made by him and his dad. But the fact was, he'd never really mastered climbing it, he didn't actually like heights, he used to wobble about wildly, his brothers used to laugh at him. He sighed.

'The whole thing was a total humiliation. It made me feel like the runt of the litter. I suppose I was, actually. Do you remember that feeling when you're twelve or thirteen, when you think everybody else is good at something and you're the only person in the world who can't do it?'

All the time he was saying this stuff, I was wondering if I was going to invite him to sit down and have a coffee, but then when he said that last bit, I decided I wasn't. I muttered something about seeing him on Wednesday, and when he'd gone, I sank back in the plastic chair and wrapped myself in my old cardigan against the cold and closed my eyes. Remembering.

There's a big bunch of them, straggling down the road, talking in loud raucous voices and pushing and jostling each other and laughing. They've got the whole pavement. I'm hurrying for the bus, I'm late for school, but I can't fight my way through all these Rushfield kids. I scuttle across the road, away from the hot blast of their laughter. Furtively I look back at them, hoping they won't see me in my Clairmont blazer, navy blue and dowdy, and those godawful grey tights. And clutching a music case. None of them have music cases. They have sports bags and school bags, pink, grubby white, purple, zingy blue and silver, covered with stickers. We're not allowed stickers. They all have their top shirt buttons undone, and their stripy ties are knotted in a wide, flaunting bulge, it uses up most of the tie, there's just a wee straggly bit hanging down. They only look like second years but already there are couples, boys and girls holding hands, skinny twelve and thirteen year olds playing at being the kids from something on TV. Grange Hill, *maybe.*

I glance across the road at them, appalled, fascinated. Then I see her. Sandra Gilroy, taller and skinnier than she was the last time I saw her, at that Leavers' Assembly at primary school, when she still wasn't speaking to me. It's a year and a half ago. Now she's wearing make-up, even from across the road I can see her blue eye shadow and her immense curly eyelashes, are they fake? And is she wearing a padded bra, to make her white school shirt bulge out like that? My chest's still as flat as an ironing board, it's mortifying.

And she's with a boy. A whole head taller than her, and spotty. He's got his arm round her shoulders, and even I, massively self-absorbed and unobservant at thirteen, can see how extremely awkward it looks. But I can also see that something's been achieved. She's got a boyfriend. And I, at my all-girl grammar school, have embarrassingly failed to connect with any of the groups: the sporty group. The pop music group. The bookish group. Or any of the other, apparently totally rigid groups at Clairmont. And if I don't get in with a group, how am I going to get invited to people's houses, how am I ever going to meet any boys?

My bus is coming. I scurry along the opposite pavement, going as fast as I can so I can get ahead of the group, cross in front of them, catch the bus. But the boy she's with suddenly jerks her round, messing about, pretending to push her off the pavement. She shoves him back, her head swoops round, just for a moment her eyes meet mine and they widen as if she's seen a ghost. Which is what I am. She's so real, so vivid, so totally here-and-now, and I'm a pale wee ghost, someone she used to hang out with years ago, but who barely exists any more. 'Hi Sandra, it's me,' I say, pathetically – because how could she even hear me, with all that traffic noise? She doesn't acknowledge my presence in any way, just drags her boyfriend across the pavement and says something to the group and they all laugh.

But she recognises me. She does. I'm sure of it.

A few drops of rain began to fall. The sky turned grey quite suddenly, clouds bulking up out of nowhere. The neighbour's cat slunk across the grass and headed for shelter, and all around me I could hear blackbirds scolding. Then a car door slammed. Roisin was back already: time to go in and make tea.

She was humming the theme from *The Moomins*. She dumped her rucksack right in the middle of the floor, and we went through the motions of the usual argument about this.

I asked 'Was it a good day?' and she said,

'Yeah, great, we went to the park and we fed the ducks, but then it got a bit boring, we went home and were just playing in the garden. Dad's garden would be really good for a high ropes course, but all they wanted to do was float things in the paddling pool and splash each other. Mum, can Denzil stay for a bit longer on Tuesday?'

I said, 'Maybe, well, you can ask him, well, you can ask his Mum.'

⋆

But when she came in from school on Tuesday, she had lost all interest in Denzil.

'Mum! Guess what! Crystal invited me to her party!'

She was ferreting in the kitchen drawer. She came out with sellotape, scissors, a roll of red tissue paper and, finally, the box with its crumpled yellow paper and orange ribbon. She was unwrapping it before I could stop her.

'It's on a boat. On the Lagan. An actual boat. Can I give her this?'

And there it was, swinging from her hot, sweaty hands: a little, sparkly blue bird, spinning round and round and catching the light, like a mobile you put up to entertain a baby, I almost expected it to start playing a tune.

'No, I'd rather you didn't.'

'Oh.' She put on a sulky look. 'Why?'

Why, indeed? Because it seemed tainted, somehow. Already rejected by one little girl. Giving it to another one seemed sort of ill-omened, or something. Or maybe I was just jealous? Roisin could keep her friends, or change her friends, as much as she wanted; they were pretty much all going to the same school. But me, I lost my best friend and never really got another one before teenage angst kicked in. I should have been glad Roisin wouldn't have to go through all that. But inside me was a whingeing eleven year old saying, *It's not fair*.

I practically grabbed the wee thing off her. There was almost a tussle; if she hadn't let go when she did, the chain probably would have snapped, and it would have ended up in the bin. But it didn't, and I got it off her, and I was standing there holding it up to the light to see if it was still OK, when Alex walked in.

She stopped in the doorway. Her hand flew up to her mouth, then fell away again.

She said, 'Oh my God. I can't believe you kept it.'

I drew in a deep breath, let it out again. There was silence in the kitchen. A baffled silence. Alex and I were gazing at each other intently, as if we'd never seen each other before.

Then I said, 'Denzil, Roisin, no coaching today. You guys go out and play, go on, you've got an hour.'

Denzil was beaming, Roisin still looking sulky, but I gave her one sharp look and out she went. All this time, Alex never took her eyes off the fragile sparkly blue bird in my hand. When they'd gone, she advanced very slowly. She lifted it out of my hands carefully. Took a step backwards.

'I wore it all night, you know. In bed. Where no-one could see me. Then in the morning I put it back in the box, and wrapped it up, and left it on your doorstep on my way to school. Yes. That's what I did. And you kept it.'

'You're . . . Sandra? You're Sandra Gilroy? You can't be, you don't . . . you don't look like her. Like Sandra.'

She took another step backwards, still cradling the necklace. Surveyed me.

'Well, you don't look much like Vinny. Thirty years have left their mark, haven't they? Though at least you still have the same nose. Mine got upgraded, a few years back. It's a much more painful operation than you'd think.'

I felt the nausea rising up into my throat. I wrinkled my whole face up and gulped it back down again.

She said, 'Don't you remember how the other kids used to tease me? About my big nose?'

'No. You didn't have a big nose. It was me who got teased. For being fat.'

'We both got teased. But we stuck up for each other. Didn't we?'

Between us there's a gap. Several paces. Thirty years. A jumble of school bags, crumbs on the floor, piles of eleven-plus papers. She stands looking across at me, like a lost little girl. Or like a deaf old person, bewildered, not understanding what's going on. She's forty-something, halfway between the lost little girl and the deaf old lady. It's not going to be enough if I just throw some words across at her, they may not reach her, they may just fall and crumble on the kitchen floor. I've got to go to her, walk across this mess and actually go to her.

So I just reached across and hugged her. For a moment it seemed an impossible thing to do. Then it seemed like the most natural thing in the world. The hug didn't seem to bear any relation to the eleven year olds we once were. Eleven year olds don't hug, not like this – eleven year olds are flimsy, wriggly, intense, easily excited, easily cowed, swayed about by life. This was two fortyish women hugging, feeling each other's solidity. Inhaling the smell of perfume, sweat, nerves, resilience; the aroma of two different homes, two different lives. Forty year olds are a steadily beating heart under an accretion of layers, they have gathered, constructed, created, survived. Hugging, sighing, patting each other's backs. I could feel hers, stiff and slippery with the silky sheen of money, she could probably feel mine sagging with exhaustion like a clapped-out sofa.

Then a glass of wine seemed like the thing, but I didn't have any, so I made instant coffee and poured a slug of brandy into each cup. And then we toasted each other. At least she did. She clinked cups with me and said 'To friendship', so of course I had to say it too and clink back, even though my stomach was churning. Embarrassment. Queasiness. Old, half-buried, half-dried-out anger.

She said, 'Are you still seething?'

'What . . . I don't know . . . it was so long ago . . . '

The brandy was making my eyes water. I must have looked like I was brimming over with emotion.

'When I think back to primary school,' she said, 'all I can remember is how bereaved I felt. Losing my best friend.'

'But you didn't have to! There were months of school left. Why did you stop speaking to me in February?'

'Who can tell what festers in the mind of a ten year old? You and I were always neck and neck, always getting Bs, week after week, month after month. I just assumed we'd be together forever, going to the same big school, I was shit scared actually, but I knew I'd always have you by my side. And then what happened? You got an A and I got a C, and my world fell apart. I'll never forget it, that phone call, you rattling on and on – "I got an A, my Mum and Dad are over the moon, I'm getting a trampoline" – and when I said I got a C, you kept saying, "No you can't have" – and then going on about your bloody trampoline again—'

'God, I was so insensitive, wasn't I?'

'Nah,' she said, 'not really. Just a typical eleven year old.'

She licked the teaspoon in her cup, slurping down the last instant-coffee-with–brandy sludge.

'And I was a typical ten year old. I could only cope by pretending: *Who cares about Vinny anyway?* I had to get new friends, fast. Friends who were going to Rushfield.'

'That seems to have worked.'

'Yeah, when I had my eleventh birthday, there were eight girls at my house, counting me. Every single girl in my class who didn't get into grammar school. We were going to a school where you didn't get three hours' homework a night, and you didn't have to wear a stupid pleated skirt over your shorts when you did PE, and you didn't have to go and sing hymns in chapel, and you didn't have to do double science and French and German, and you didn't have to go to rugby matches and cheer on the boys.'

She sighed.

'And then my mum came in with your present, and the other girls said, "Oh, that's from stuck-up Vinny, it's really old-fashioned looking, it's like something your granny would get you!" But I thought it was beautiful.'

'So why didn't you keep it?' I asked her.

We'd moved to sit side by side on the sofa, with our backs to the kitchen window so we couldn't see the devastation the kids were wreaking in the garden. She was running the silver chain through her fingers, turning the little blue glass swallow round and round so it kept catching the light. On the wall beside the fireplace, rainbow specks were appearing and disappearing, depending which way she turned it.

She started telling me a long, rambling story about breaking her kitchen window with a football when she was a wee tomboy of nine, and running through the house and out into the street, hunkering down and trying to hide behind her brother's bike. And her mum came and hauled her back in and made her sweep up the glass, and she was furious, and her dad came in and said No point crying over spilt milk, and it wasn't as if she'd done it on purpose. Then her mum and dad had a row, and that was almost worse than her mum being cross with just her. And it put her right off football, for weeks she couldn't look at a football, she couldn't even go into the kitchen, and if she had to, she tried really, really hard not to look at the window. As if not looking at it would make the whole painful, embarrassing experience go away.

'And then,' she went on, 'it was the same with this wee bird. I was so full of anger and guilt and sadness and – oh, defiance, I suppose – masses of conflicting emotions. They all came rushing up fit to choke me, every time I looked at this wee thing. There was like a force field emanating from it, nowhere in our house or our yard was big enough to keep that force away from me. The only way I could deal with the whole thing was to squash all those emotions back in the box and wrap it up and take it somewhere far, far away. So that's why I left it on your doorstep. It was like burying it.'

She gave a bit of a forced grin, wrinkling up that new nose of hers, and said 'Can I put it on?'

'Of course. It's yours. If it doesn't mind. I mean if your other stuff doesn't mind having this, you know, kind of gatecrasher in your jewellery box.'

'Oh lord, I have a different jewellery box for every day of the week, Derek always gives me loads of stuff, but this – this has its own wee box and I'm going to keep it locked away where Derek nor nobody else can't find it.'

As I turned round to clasp it behind the back of her neck, I saw Roisin in the kitchen doorway, staring at us. Her eyes widened, and she opened her mouth to ask . . .I stopped her.

'No. Don't ask. Absolutely not. You know you have stuff about your friends, that you wouldn't tell your Mum? Well, it works the other way round, too.'

'No, I just wanted to know is it time for tea yet? Because I'm starving.'

We both laughed. Alex and me.

She said, 'Can you believe it? Six o'clock already. Go and tell Denzil we're leaving in five minutes.'

As Roisin flashed off, shooting us a hard-to-read look, I asked, 'When did you turn into Alex?'

'Oh,' she said, 'I was actually christened Alexandra. After my granny. Of course it got shortened to Sandra. After my aunty. Alex was never used, it was a snooker player's name, not a girl's name, so yeah, I guess I took it up after I left home. After I started nursing. Everything got upgraded, first my name, then my nose . . . now there isn't anything much left to work on.'

And then we both said, at the same time, 'Except Denzil'.

That felt really, really weird.

She asked if she could bring him for a session on Friday, because Derek had started asking how the sessions were going, so he'd know this one hadn't happened. In fact, she went on, Derek could bring him, because he'd actually told her he was off on Friday afternoon, whereas Fridays they stayed open till four at Lunch at Louisa's. Not that she was telling Derek that, of course –

'Of course,' I said, not really understanding what she meant, and then she said, 'On Saturday, let's go somewhere! It's May Day, isn't it? Take a picnic, dump the kids in a really high-powered playground, then we can talk and talk—'

'Playground?'

'Yeah, you haven't got much more playground time with Roisin, pretty soon she'll be turning up her nose at all that – my Chloe thought playgrounds were *so* yesterday's breakfast by the time she was twelve. Pity, because you can actually get them out in the sunshine and then you can ignore them for a couple of hours.'

And then, as she and Denzil were leaving, she hugged me again, and Roisin's eyes widened even further. I put frozen pizzas in the oven, and thought how I really didn't want to talk about any of this weird business with anyone under forty, but I needn't have worried, all Roisin wanted to know was, what could she give Crystal for her birthday, now that the necklace had gone?

On Wednesday, after school, I had to accompany Roisin to a gift shop on the Lisburn Road; two extra bus journeys and that took up some of my marking time, because I had all the Easter maths tests to do. So on Thursday I was marking till midnight. And on Friday, when Roisin was away with Crystal for hours on end, I had Denzil after school for an hour. I don't know which of us was dopier, him or me.

So I'd hardly had a moment to think about Alex/Sandra/Alexandra, the strangeness of it. It reminded me of a rose bush my Granny once had, that had got kind of hybridised somewhere along the line, so it put out two sorts of flowers, one lustrous and cultivated and dewy, the other with thin, sparse petals, like a dog rose growing in the hedgerow. While Denzil was struggling with some particularly intransigent problems involving areas in square metres of oddly shaped, unsquare rooms, I found myself looking round my dusty, scruffy kitchen, that had never been properly repainted since the builders came and knocked the two rooms into one, and remembering how she'd said, 'I just wanted to see where you lived.'

Derek, meanwhile, was sitting in the car. He was doing something important-looking on his iPad, and I remembered Denzil sitting in the car with his Nintendo, the first time he was at my house. Was it really only six weeks ago? And he'd had to come in, because it had run out of juice. I hoped Derek's i-Pad wouldn't run out.

Actually he looked as if he'd run out of juice himself. He looked sort of dry and desiccated, with his neatly groomed sandy/grey hair getting a bit thin on top, as if the sun had been too much for it and it had started to shrivel up. I'd known he must be a bit older than her, but I hadn't expected him to look so worn and tired.

He came in at the end and asked, 'Has this young man been working hard for you today?'

'Of course,' I replied, wearily.

'Good to hear it,' he said. 'Denzil, go and wait in the car would you, please?'

I thought, here it comes, the inquisition about why my own child isn't going to grammar school, this is going to be embarrassing, and it's half past four on Friday afternoon, I'm just not up to this, I'm exhausted.

But he only asked, quite mildly, 'So, I gather you're in favour of integrated education?'

I said, 'Yes, Roisin's dad is a Catholic' and he said, 'Ah, of course, I see,' and got off the subject quickly, as if he'd touched on something slightly emotional or embarrassing, like a family bereavement, or the sudden discovery that one of us had had a nervous breakdown ten years ago.

It turned out what he really wanted was to talk about plans for the summer. How many sessions a week would Denzil need? When was I going on holiday? Would it be best to give him a break then, or should they keep him at it? One of his colleague's sons was going to a sports camp, ten AM till four PM, did I think this would do Denzil good, or would it tire him out and stop him concentrating on his work? And then there was the Cub camp, obviously that would be extremely tiring, no two ways about it, but it was only a long weekend, so presumably it wouldn't do any harm?

I pulled myself together.

'No, it's fine. Plenty of fresh air, plenty of exercise, it's the summer, he'll work all the better if he has wee breaks.'

I was deliberately avoiding eye contact. No amount of breaks and no amount of keeping him at it would do any good. He was almost certainly going to get the current equivalent of a C, or even a D if he had a couple of bad days and most of the other kids didn't . His parents would need to start thinking, if he didn't get into grammar school, what were their options? And if he did just scrape in, how much coaching was he going to need for the next seven years, to keep up with the others? All this, he would see in my face, if we looked at each other. So I made sure we didn't. I shuffled papers and tried to look busy. In fact, I tried to look more like Derek than Derek. I wasn't going to have this conversation with him. I was going to have it with Alex, or Sandra, or whatever her name was. After all, she was his mother. She hadn't been mentioned once, had she?

And so I thought about her all evening. There was a text from Roisin, to say the party had started late, and the boat had to go all the way up from Stranmillis to the docks and then out all round the *Titanic* area and they were getting a tour of where the *Titanic* was built and then they were having their tea in the café at the actual *Titanic* centre and if Crystal's Mum was going to run her home, it would be at least another two hours, and did I mind?

Mind? I sank back on the sofa. I ate a Pot Noodle because I was too tired to cook. I gazed out the window at the last evening of April, the sky a thoughtful sad kind of violet-grey, and all the new leaves, that had come out in the last couple of days, a mad wavering flaring green, like hundreds of butterflies quivering against the greyness.

I thought about friendship. If we'd stayed friends, me and Sandra, if we'd gone up to Clairmont together, in that harsh stultifying new environment we'd have clung to each other like scared kittens. But then after a year or so, we might have drifted apart, nothing in common any more, it happens all the time. So if we'd met again after thirty years or so, it wouldn't be such a big deal, would it?

Well – maybe. But some people keep their childhood friends for life. I don't know if that's better, or worse. Perhaps it just means that both your lives haven't changed that much. Actually, I thought, mine hasn't. You could have pretty well predicted I'd become a primary school teacher. I might have been living in a slightly bigger house, that's all. And I look just like you'd think a fortysomething Vinny would look. But her – she's completely re-invented herself – she must have worked so hard.

Having a nose job. Surgery. An actual operation. With an anaesthetic and coming round feeling sick. Being sick, maybe, into one of those kidney-shaped bowls made of greyish paper that you hold to your cheek because you're going to vomit and you haven't got the strength to sit up. And not being able to breathe properly. Would you have to have a tube in your nose? Would there be stuff to drain away? Aargh. It must have been disgusting. And sore. Did she do it before or after she had the kids? I bet Stewart and Chloe have got noses which, like Denzil's, are so utterly normal that no-one would look at them twice. I hope so, anyway. Because you wouldn't put a young person through that, when they're in their late teens, early twenties, trying to find themselves, to find out about what sort of person they are, what they want to do with their lives – would you? Poor wee soul. She must have had such low self-esteem. She must have been desperate.

When Roisin came back, with her party bag of sweets and tacky *Titanic* souvenirs, and bursting with the information that Crystal had nearly fallen into the water during the boat trip, I just said 'You know that wee necklace? I did actually give it to Denzil's Mum.'

'Do you mean now? Or when you and her were kids, you gave it to her?'

'Both. I gave it to her when she was your age, and she wouldn't take it because she was cross with me, and then on Tuesday I gave it to her again, and this time she's going to keep it.'

'Does that mean she's not cross with you any more?'

'That's right. She's not.'

'So that's good, isn't it? Are you happy?'

'Of course,' I said. 'Yeah. Of course I am. Of course I'm happy.'

MAY

But it didn't mean I wasn't nervous. Saturday morning, there I was, suddenly stuck in a car for the best part of an hour with a person I hardly knew, and a person who had been my best mate thirty years ago. And they were the same person. What was I supposed to talk about? And that pair in the back, listening to every word.

We drove past this crumpled up thing, draped from a lamp post.

'What's that flag doing here?' said Roisin suspiciously.

It was a very large Union Jack, must have been double the usual size, on a lamp post at the corner of our street, perched right at the top of all the election posters.

The impression the lamp post gave was that the TUV could climb higher than the DUP, the SDLP could climb higher than the TUV, UKIP could climb higher than the SDLP and the Union Jack could climb higher than the lot of them.

At least there wasn't any wind, so it wasn't flapping at us, just hanging limp. In a moment we were past, but no-one could let the subject drop.

'That's a bit in-your-face, isn't it?' said Alex/Sandra. 'Still more than two months to the Twelfth. Starting a bit early, aren't they?'

'It's the first time ever,' I said, and started explaining how when I was house hunting, seven years ago, I'd made a point of going round in July, at the height of the marching season, to make sure there were no flags festering in the street I was moving into. And up to this moment, there never had been.

'Are Union Jacks not a good thing to have?' asked Denzil. 'Only the Cubs have one and the Scouts and . . . '

'Catholic Cubs and Scouts and Brownies and Guides don't have Union Jacks,' Roisin asserted.

Denzil gazed at her in amazement. 'What?'

'Catholic Cubs and Scouts and . . . '

'Denzil doesn't know what Catholic Cubs are,' Alex explained. 'In fact,' she added wickedly, 'I'm not sure he knows what Catholics are, do you, son?'

But Roisin was in full flood.

'We're doing a project on flags at school. Britain has the Union Jack and in Northern Ireland some people like it and some people don't and Ireland has the tricolour and in Northern Ireland some people like it and some people don't and some people get a wee bit confused, because it's almost the same as the flag of Italy. I wish we were doing a project on Italy.'

Denzil sighed. 'I wish we were doing a project on anything. We don't do projects in P6.'

'Why not?'

'Because of the tests.'

We were driving through Carryduff with its generous complement of Union Jacks, and Denzil brightened up.

'I could take that Union Jack down if you don't want it there. I could take all these Union Jacks down. I'm a great climber. My Cub leader says I'm descended from a long line of geckos.'

'Don't even think about it!' Alex scolded.

'Why not?'

'It would be dangerous—'

'I'm sure you don't have any flags in your street,' I said, getting tired of the whole subject.

'Oh, you must come to my house,' said Alex. 'Soon.'

We drove on through the bright May morning. All the trees were out in leaf, a cacophany of competing greens, the dandelions expiring on the verges and the bluebells beginning to show, gorse like scraps of sunshine made solid in the rocky fields, and lambs – big fat lambs, tiny tremulous lambs, bouncy ones and sleepy ones and lying-in-a-heap ones. It seemed so long since I'd been out in the country. Roisin, too. Denzil gave the impression that if you'd seen one lamb, you'd seen them all, but Roisin cooed over each and every one.

'I love animals,' she said. 'I think when I grow up, I might get a job working with animals.'

'Me too,' said Denzil instantly, not entirely convincingly.

'In my gap year,' she added thoughtfully, 'I might try it out.'

'My sister wants to have a gap year,' said Denzil cheerfully. 'My dad's raging.'

'As of this morning,' explained Alex/Sandra. 'He's investing all his mental energies in trying to convince Chloe that she'd be stone mad to take a gap year, when she's got seven years of a medical degree ahead of her. She's got three offers for medicine and she did *not* specify on her UCAS form that she wanted to take a year out. He won't be fussing so much about Denzil's progress, now that he's got a new project. Chloe's medical career. Which is a subject heactually does know something about.'

'So . . . is this just Chloe's wee token rebellion thing? This gap year idea?'

'Quite possibly. It's all been a bit tense with Chloe recently. She was out till two AM last night at some club, and during the run-up to A-levels, that's just, she put on Derek's accent . . . '*totally inappropriate*.'

'How'd she get in?'

'Borrowed some maverick eighteen year old's ID, I suppose.' Alex sighed.

'When we were that age, we didn't have any clubs to go to, did we, what with the Troubles . . . the city centre was dead at night, wasn't it? I remember, when I was in the nurses' home, way high up, sometimes at night you'd look down and see wee bits of light, like beacon fires, only it was burning cars or buses. You forget so quickly, don't you?'

Denzil and Roisin weren't listening. They were absorbed in all this stuff about gap years. Roisin was patiently explaining that if you can take a gap year *after* you go to big school, you should also be able to take one before. So she was going to take hers straight after P7. She was going to be a volunteer at the Animal Sanctuary. She'd been up there with her friend Zoe, when Zoe was getting her cat. Buster. There were lots of lovely cats, only some of them were a bit shy and scared of people, so they needed more people to talk to them. A lot. And stroke them. And there were lovely dogs, she was going to help take the dogs for walks, three times a day.

'And are you going to help clean out the cats' litter trays?' Alex asked innocently.

'Oh no,' said Roisin grandly. 'They have *staff* to do that.'

Alex and I giggled simultaneously. Roisin looked offended.

'What would you do if you had a gap year?' she asked Denzil.

'I'd go to Cub Camp. And then I'd go to Scout Camp. Because when you're ten you can go to either the Cubs or the Scouts. And then I'd go to a camp in Switzerland and climb mountains. You can do that when you're in the Explorers, when you're fourteen. But I'd make them let me do it in my Gap Year. Then I'd go as a helper on lots of other camps.'

Roisin told Denzil that she thought her plans were a bit more practical than his, and he said no they weren't, how much time can you actually spend stroking cats? Roisin said, lots of time, if there are lots of cats.

We sat peacefully in the front, listening to them argue. When you have an only child, you don't get to listen to them arguing with siblings; their only domestic adversary is yourself. And Denzil, according to Alex, was almost like an only child too, being so much younger than the others. They rambled happily on with their grandiose plans and their bickering.

Alex whispered to me, 'Do you think they really believe it?'

I whispered back, 'Maybe. Maybe they half believe it. There's a boy in my P6 class who told me he wanted to put down Hogwarts as one of his five choices for big school. But not to tell the others.'

'Because they'd laugh at him?'

'No. Because they're all muggles!'

We were giggling again, and I added, 'I think that's part of the reason Roisin likes Denzil. Because he believes everything she says.'

We turned in to the meandering drive of the Country Park, and Alex paid £4.50 at the hut without a murmur. We took the last space in the car park. The picnic tables were at the top of a slope, with the ground falling away steeply into a sort of flood plain, awash with play equipment. Alex had to literally drag Denzil back up the slope by the collar of his T-shirt.

'Eat first. Play later.'

She plied them with little round pizza bites and ham-and-mustard pinwheels and mini hazelnut brownies. Only when they were completely stuffed did she give Denzil a shove and send him rolling like a cartoon character down the hill, Roisin picking her way more carefully after him.

'We don't want them popping back all the time, bothering us for food,' she explained. 'Have some tapenade?'

I dipped a cheese stick into it. It looked homemade.

'Did you do all this yourself?'

'Lord, no,' she said. 'It's from Lunch at Louisa's, I snaffled it after work yesterday, this is what the good folks of South Belfast wouldn't eat.'

And she started pouring wine into plastic goblets.

She'd brought an actual bottle of Rose d'Anjou. The sun shone, blackbirds were warbling in the oak tree beside the picnic tables, swallows flickered round us. I noticed she was wearing the little swallow necklace again. It looked chunky and a bit too blue, compared to the real birds that were swooping and darting almost down to the grass, catching flies or just missing them, dark and skinny and nervy and always in motion.

We had a second glass of wine.

'So,' she said cheerily, 'what went wrong with your marriage then?' as if it was a given, that something was bound to go wrong with all marriages in the end.

A whole lot of stuff came gushing out when I started telling her about Rory; it seemed like years since anyone had shown so much interest in what I had to say. I told her how we'd lived together for a year, so you couldn't really say we'd rushed into getting married, could you, and yet, we were both still terribly young. And I had no concept that when you marry a guy, you marry his whole family, and he'll never be able to shake off their expectations. I was too busy fending off my own family.

Of course, I couldn't tell my mum that I was living with a fella. She was an old-fashioned lady. She kept popping round to our flat, bringing me house plants and nourishing little home-cooked meals in

Pyrex dishes. She thought I must be so tired, what with it being my first full-time teaching job. When she'd gone, Rory would emerge from the bedroom, yawning his head off, bored and sleepy, nothing to do in there except read the paper and listen to music on his Walkman, it was before the days of iPods. She wondered why she never saw my flat-mate, so I had to invent a flatmate who was out a lot, and slept on the sofa bed in the sitting room, and stored all her clothes in my wardrobe, and never left her personal belongings lying around. It was like being three or four again, and having an imaginary friend. I even gave her a name. Marietta McStay.

Rory's family were very traditional Catholics, they would have been pretty uncomfortable about the whole thing too. But they never visited. Far too busy, with all those children and the children of the children and the cousins and the children of the cousins and so on. Rory hated being kept out of my mum's way. He started to talk about getting married, and I said Rory this is ridiculous, we can't get married just to please my mum. He said, 'Don't you like me even a teeny bit then?' With that cute little boy lost look. I adored that look.

'And so you married him?' Alex was smiling. 'It was that easy?'

'Too easy. He was dying to make us an item, present me to all his brothers and sisters and uncles and aunties and . . . when my mum got to know him, she didn't approve. She thought he was a bit scatty, a bit feckless, a bit immature, a bit in need of looking after.

'All that was true, of course; it was part of his charm, for me. Everything in his life wasn't all tightly organised and controlled and buttoned up, the way it was in my parents' life. Rory was so easy-going, so easy to get along with. And he loved kids; he was great with all his nephews and nieces, he wanted a big, jolly family.

'Also he wanted a big, jolly woman to manage his family. He didn't actually want to have to take equal shares in the responsibility. He was devastated when I had a miscarriage, he was actually more upset than I was, I'd been feeling awfully sick and then at ten weeks when I lost it I actually felt physically better, it was all very confusing, I felt almost guilty, and all his family kept saying, sorry to hear you lost a wee baby, and he wanted to try again right away. I wanted to wait a bit, but trying to get Rory to use condoms was definitely a bridge too far . . . so I got pregnant again two months later.'

Alex shook her head and went tsk.

'Poor you. So you were knackered before you even had Roisin.'

She was right. I hadn't realised it at first, but I was tired out from two pregnancies, and Rory just hadn't a clue. He thought it was awful big of him to stay in on Saturday, missing out on his sporting activities just to mind a one and a half year old with a gippy tummy, so that I could go out for a swim . . . and when I came back, the place would be a tip and he wouldn't have thought to start the dinner.

But Roisin made up for it all, she was such a wee person right from the start, such a wee character. Once she started to talk, the things she said were so cute and hilarious, I didn't want to miss any of it, so I took a year off on a career break. That was the death knell of the marriage, of course. I'd spend the day entertaining Roisin and trying to have the house perfect for when he came home, and I'd burn the dinner and he'd say, never mind, sure we'll just get a takeaway, and I'd bite his head off. I wasn't the girl he'd married, I'd become a targe, an absolute targe.

But he was still the guy I'd married: young, good-looking, funny, spontaneous, warm-hearted, disorganised, optimistic, messy . . . and in need of a good woman to look after him. As well as exasperated, I felt guilty.

'I should have known what he was like,' I told Alex, 'and I should have known that I wasn't the woman he needed, and I should have known that we just weren't right for each other.'

'Yeah, sure,' said Alex. 'Why is it always the

woman who has to have self-knowledge and insight, it's all her responsibility, and the man's allowed to be as blind as a bat?'

We were sitting on the rug, leaning up against the bole of the oak tree. The wine was finished. The sun had come round till it was in our eyes, and I had no sunglasses, so I was squinting against the glare. I thought: Could you picture Derek as a bat? Not really. Right enough, his face was quite foxy, but his eyes weren't blind, they were alarmingly shrewd. Piercing blue eyes, isn't that what they say?

And I thought about Rory again, and I wondered, *Why isn't there more sadness?* Looking back down the years, all I can remember is the relief. When I went back to teaching, and I used to go and pick up Roisin from the nursery at four o'clock and she'd be prattling away about stuff she'd done and showing me wee things she'd made, and we'd go to the park and then go home and put the dinner on, and it was all so much simpler without Rory coming in and me expecting him to do things. I just did them myself. I was happier, calmer on my own, without Rory. It had been a lovely roaring winter log fire, and it had burnt itself out. Isn't that a tragedy in itself? Shouldn't it feel tragic, even looking back?

But all I could feel, sitting there on the hard, bumpy ground with one leg gone to sleep under me, was awkwardness. I'd just poured out all the bad stuff from my marriage, from years ago, to a more or less total stranger. Because that's what she was, surely? The fact that we'd been best friends, thirty odd years ago, didn't mean we'd have anything in common now – or that I could actually trust her. What if she went and relayed all this stuff about my past to that cardboard husband of hers? Or what if I asked her, 'Tell me about your marriage then', and she just said, as well she might, 'Oh, let's not talk about Derek'? And I'd given her everything, and she was going to give me nothing?

I stood up and gazed down over the playground. Roisin saw me, and came frisking up.

'We've just seen some swallows and can we have an ice cream?'

'The swallows,' Denzil explained earnestly, 'are catching wee tiny flies. There's a sort of muddy patch and it's got flies and they're flying right down over it, really low. My Cub leader says, when the swallows fly low, it's a sign it's going to rain.'

'Great,' said Alex. 'Better grab some ice creams and get back in the playground quick, before it starts to pour.'

She casually handed Denzil a five pound note, as if it was just a wee crumpled piece of paper she'd found in her pocket.

'We're away for a big scenic walk,' she told him. 'Half an hour, no more. You guys go straight to the shop then back to the playground and we expect to see you there, OK? No wandering off.'

I watched Denzil lolloping off and Roisin haring after him. 'Will they know where to go?'

'Oh yeah,' she said, 'I bring him here with his mates from school sometimes. Used to be, if they got really tired and whingey, I'd send them up to the shop for ice creams to pacify them. Now it's more like, if one of them gets injured at football.'

We trudged up the hill, me struggling to keep up with her, parodying Roisin chugging after Denzil. I asked if Denzil wouldn't prefer to be here with his mates, rather than Roisin? She said she thought Roisin might be turning into a sort of substitute sister. Chloe, who was naturally a bit bossy and scornful, was nasty as a bag of cats these days, with her A-levels coming up. She didn't have much time for Denzil.

Also,' she added, 'deep down, though it isn't macho to admit it, he possibly prefers playgrounds to football.'

The walk was a good idea: a bit of sobering up was called for. There was a fresh breeze, making the leaves rustle as we passed horse chestnuts already flourishing their white candles. The grass was long, starred with flowers I didn't know the names of, and Denzil's swallows were swishing and swooping past us.

I hadn't walked up a steep hill for ages; I was

getting out of breath, and it made it harder to ask, 'So how did you fall for Derek?'

At first she didn't answer. I thought, *She thinks I'm being intrusive, and she's going to go back to being Mrs Masterton. And that'll be the end of it.*

Then she said, 'Actually I didn't.'

'Sorry?'

'I didn't fall for him. To be honest. I really, really convinced myself I was in love with him. But actually . . . well, when I was sixteen, I just scraped into a school with a sixth form, to do A-levels, and then I just scraped into nursing, of course you didn't need a degree for nursing in those days, and then when I met him, this handsome final-year medical student, surrounded as he was by high-powered attractive female medical students, it was touch and go, but I just managed to scrape into a relationship with him.

'Wow. It was such an achievement. In fact he'd actually been going out with a medical student, called Melanie, she was a real high flyer but she. . . he said she was always tired. Pre-occupied. Final-year medicine: they were both under such pressure. They were having a lot of rows. So I just made sure I was always available, fresh and glossy, never tired compared to Melanie, I was so relaxing for him to be with.'

'Yes, I can understand how . . . but why?'

'Why,' she said.

We had reached the top of the hill, and I flopped down on to a bench, Alex perching beside me, swinging her legs and thinking. As if the question had never occurred to her before. A frown on her face, as she watched the white sails of the boats scudding to and fro across Strangford Lough below us.

She said slowly, 'I was probably bound to fall in love with a doctor. Do you know, when I was Denzil's age, I actually wanted to *be* a doctor? But you couldn't be a doctor if you'd been at Rushfield. Obviously. Doctors had such a glamour, you know. Well, not the ones in our local practice, they were all ancient. But the ones you saw on TV . . . '

She gave a sad laugh.

'I was only nineteen.'

'So . . . '

I was trying to find a sensitive way to ask, Did you honestly only fall in love with him because he was going to be a doctor? But there was no sensitive way. So I just went ahead and asked it. She swished her long, sun-tanned legs. She sighed.

'All the boys I knew at school were such messers. Even some of the medical students, when I started nursing. But Derek, he was ambitious and dynamic and a wee bit ruthless. He was such a driven person. Can you believe it, both his parents were consultants? Whatever Derek does, he does one hundred percent. And he doesn't suffer fools gladly. Everybody knows exactly what he expects of them. I found it kind of reassuring.'

She fell silent, and we listened to the seagulls calling down on the lough shore and some little bird twittering in the long grass near us, unseen. I wondered if it had a nest.

Eventually she said, 'It wears off, of course.'

'What does?'

'That reassuring feeling. That he expects absolutely the best from everyone, and that's exactly what he's going to get, and so everybody knows where they are and everything's OK. After a while, it just gets a bit wearing, like having your school headmaster making a speech at you every morning. Only he doesn't actually have to put it into words. It gets a wee bit tiring in the end.'

'Alex, you are the least tired person I know! Look at you striding up these hills, I can't keep up with you!'

'It's true,' she admitted. 'I used to be up before seven to be on the wards by eight thirty, facing a killer day. I can still remember how grim that was. The thought of not having to do it any more, wow, that really gives you an energy boost. Even years later.'

She stretched and grinned.

'Course, I've always been a bouncy sort of person. For the last twenty years I've been having to tone myself down a bit.'

She jumped off the bench.

'OK, down the hill, I'll race you! I'll give you a start of a count of ten, come on, I'm counting, one, two—'

It was like being bossed about in the playground by her, when we were little. But it's been a long time since anyone bossed me about, so I ran, with the wind in my ears and my heart pounding and my handbag thumping off my hip and half strangling me round my neck and the distant screaming of the seagulls coasting across on the warm air currents, barely reaching me above the noise of pounding feet. Halfway-down, she suddenly stopped. There was a sort of pond, brackish and infested with midges, but she pulled off her trainers and waded straight in, gasping at the coldness. Then sighing with pleasure.

'God, it feels like years since I've had my bare toes in the water . . . '

'Don't you ever go to the beach?'

'Oh yes – a whole crowd of us used to go to Donegal, sometimes Hallowe'en, sometimes Easter, tramping along Rosapenna Strand—'

'And don't you ever paddle?'

'Well, no. Bare feet are for the pool, you see, the hotel pool. Trainers are what you wear for the beach.'

She splashed a few times then waded out, flecks of mud on her immaculate beige linen shorts, and while she was putting her trainers back on I set off running again.

This time I had a long enough start to let me arrive, puffing and gasping, back at the playground just before she did.

'I let you win.'

'No you didn't.'

'Yes I did.'

We were showing off for the benefit of Denzil and Roisin, who were sitting on a picnic table looking up at us in amazement.

I flopped down beside them.

'Mum, you don't usually run,' Roisin complained.

'She doesn't have time,' said Alex. 'Running's for when you're young and free.'

'I am free,' I said. 'Only I waste my free time sitting gazing up at the sky.'

Even as I was speaking, the sky was turning grey and raindrops were starting to fall, randomly at first, then persistently. Alex chivvied the children into the car. They were damp and tired out, and on the way home we actually sang, the way my family used to sing to cheer up long car journeys when I was very young. It's true that I don't run much, but I do still sing, and if I had a car, I'd sing in it with Roisin. For another few months at least, before it became uncool, before she would start refusing to turn off her iPod and take those wee things out of her ears for anything less than a major emergency. We sang *Ten green bottles* and *The Bog Down in the*

Valley-O and then, causing Roisin and Denzil and ourselves major embarrassment, we sang *Climb Every Mountain* from *The Sound of Music*. Alex claimed that we used to sing it in the choir at primary school, with Miss Elstree conducting. I remembered Miss Elstree as a frightful nag, though Alex said I was one of her favourites. We reminisced about all the teachers, who was fun and who was sometimes fun and who was totally unfair, and Denzil stared out of the window, obviously bored, but I could see Roisin was riveted. When your mum is a teacher, the idea that she once had teachers, nice ones and cross ones and shouting ones, is slightly subversive. Slightly disturbing.

It stopped raining, but there were traffic jams on the way back to Belfast, and we sang some more, until Alex started to run out of steam. She was worrying about the time, and trying to remember when she'd said she'd be back, so I told her, 'Don't bother coming into the street; just drop us at the corner.' Under the gaze of some local boys kicking a football across the road and back, Roisin and Denzil barely said goodbye to each other. They both managed a sort of countryman's nod – wordless recognition but no eye contact.

What I'd taken for an ice cream van, parked near our house, turned out to be Locally Organic. The veg man emerged from it with a box of dusty looking veg, a bunch of bananas draped across the top. I remembered Alex's comment about bananas not being local. I gave him the same sort of nod that Roisin and Denzil had just given each other. Roisin was a few paces ahead, then she came darting back to me.

'I saw a swallow!' Her wee face was all lit up. 'Look! There's another one!'

Way up in the grey-blue sky above our street, thin streamlined birds with sickle-shaped wings were soaring and swooping, making a faint high-pitched screeching noise. They didn't look like swallows to me. They weren't blue; they were dark, almost black. Their distant curving flight stirred a vague memory in me.

'Those are swallows,' Roisin pleaded, 'aren't they?'

'Well, no,' said the veg man, apologetically. 'You mostly get swallows where there's water, and the right kind of insects. They're country fellas. These ones here are swifts; they're the ones that come into cities.'

'Why are they screeching?' she asked.

'Who knows? Maybe they're saying, look at me, look how high I can fly—'

She shook her head disbelievingly.

He continued, 'That's one way you know they aren't swallows. Swallows twitter. Also, they don't fly so high. These guys nest in church spires, really high buildings, that's why they like cities.'

It came back to me: that sort of half-fledged memory. It was the time Rory and I went inter-railing, and we fetched up in Siena with no money, and had an argument over whether it would be safe to try to sleep in a doorway, or in a courtyard under some arches, and would the stone pavements still be warm with the searing heat of the day? And there, around the ridiculously high tower of the Palazzo Pubblico, those same birds were soaring and swooping. Black, and with great big long wings. Even in the dusk we could still hear them, it was late August and it was like they were saying, summer's gone, we have to go, fly away! Fly away! Fly away!

'It's May,' I said. 'Why aren't they on their nests?'

'Ah, they're on their nests alright. These are just the harassed fathers. Getting insects to feed the mothers and babies. Very responsible. Later on you'll hear a lot more noise and carry-on, when the young ones are fledged, there'll be gangs of teenage swifts roaming the skies and screaming their heads off.' Roisin was scraping her feet on the ground with boredom. 'Can we have pizza tonight?'

I gave her the keys, and told her to run in and put the oven on. I stood in the street with the veg man, listening to the swifts, thinking of Siena nearly twenty years ago. The high-pitched screaming brought back the sensations I had then: hunger, light-headedness, worry, exhilaration. And that intense, exhausting heat; I've never felt it since.

'I see there's a flag up in your street,' the veg man remarked. 'Never seen that before.'

'Yes, it's always been pretty non-sectarian and quiet here,' I said. 'I suppose it's because of all the flag protests, City Hall and all that. Oh, it makes me so angry.'

Though it didn't, really. More sort of exasperated and tired.

'I could take that flag down for you,' he offered.

'Oh, I couldn't let you. Too dangerous.'

He grinned. 'I'm too old to fall out of trees.'

'No, I mean, if they knew who it was, and if they found out where you lived, they could come round and get you. That's why nobody takes these flags down. That's why the council workers won't touch them.'

'Sure, I know all that,' he said. 'But I'll come round tomorrow morning. Half past nine. Even the churchgoers won't be up, and as for the UVF, I don't think half past nine on Sunday morning is their natural habitat, do you?'

I asked him, would he normally be up that early on a Sunday himself, and he said yes because Sunday was the only day he didn't deliver, so if it was sunny, he was up with the dawn working in the veg garden. I said it sounded idyllic, and he groaned.

And of course I didn't expect him to turn up, but there he was next morning at nine thirty on the button, saying it would help a lot if I could hold the ladder, but of course, not to, if I was worried anyone would see me.

I glanced up and down the street. No-one. I held the ladder and closed my eyes as he stood on the very top rung, straining up to reach, with what looked like a very sharp pair of pruning secateurs, to snip the thin plastic stuff that held the flag round the pole. The flag gave a helpless sort of shudder and slithered down more or less on top of me, and I nearly got pinged in the eye by one of the thin whippy bits of plastic, that were like the stuff Bord na Móna puts round the peat briquettes.

'Sorry, Missis, I didn't mean to engulf you in a flag.'

'Please don't call me Missis, it's Vinny.'

'Oh,' he said, and looked totally embarrassed, and didn't think to tell me his name.

'Anyway,' I said, 'I thought you were scared of climbing?'

He grinned. 'Well, it's a good thing you didn't point that out two minutes ago. Now that I'm down, I can say that, yes, I am. But this isn't a rope ladder, and actually, it's not so bad when your big brothers aren't watching you.'

Then there was the problem of what to do with the flag. At this point I got a text from Alex, to say could she bring Denzil tomorrow instead of Tuesday? I texted back to say, Sure, and had she any suggestions about what to do with a Union Jack I suddenly seemed to have on my hands? No answer. The veg man bundled it up, and said it would be safest in his compost bins, nobody would track it down there.

'Flag protests may come and flag protests may go,' he asserted, 'but this flag is destined to end its days as compost.'

We both gave a little, satisfied sigh. I could see he was very pleased with himself. At this point, a text came back from Alex:

> Flag? Well, you could make it into a hammock for the garden, pretend it came from the Cath Kidston shop. Or Denzil and Roisin could have it as part of the assault course maybe . . .

The veg man didn't seem to think either of these suggestions was helpful, or funny. He said my friend Mrs Masterton seemed to have a slightly off-kilter sense of humour.

I told this to Alex, next day after the session, when the kids were trying to work out how to get from the trampoline to the apple tree without killing themselves, and we were nibbling macaroons she'd snaffled from Lunch at Louisa's. Sweet, slightly sickly puffs of flavoured air.

'He seemed to get a bit frosty when I mentioned you,' I said.

'Oh Lord, he would, I guess.'

'Why?'

'Well. It's like this. I'm fairly sure Derek's been seeing someone.'

I thought, Oh for the love of Mike, what am I supposed to say, but it was alright because I didn't have to say anything except 'Mmm.' She just rattled on and on, obviously feeling totally at ease with me, that she didn't have to put up a front, I was her oldest friend, wasn't I?

'I'm sure it's happened before. Maybe a couple of times. He's out so much and so long: it couldn't possibly be work. Of course, he claims it is. And he actually seems a wee bit less spiky, more relaxed, that's how I know . . . '

'You didn't just come straight out and ask him?'

'Lord, no. Of course he wouldn't tell me, anyway. He'd just go all frosty and formal, as if I was an ex-patient making an unfounded complaint. Anyway, I'm not seriously worried. He's not going to do anything to upset the apple cart. He can't do without me. He knows he can't. So it just leaves me free to . . . well . . . to do anything I want. Really. Doesn't it?'

She smiled her brave, brittle smile. Started telling me about the veg man, whose name was Chris, apparently. (*Yes,* I thought, *Chris suits him: a terse, practical, no-frills sort of name. a bit sunburnt and dusty.*) And she said he wasn't just someone who delivered veg, he actually had a degree in horticulture, he knew everything about stuff that grew, he'd been so helpful, last summer, going round the garden with her and giving her advice . . . So naturally, she'd assumed . . . It was a scorching hot day, and he came into the sun room and had a gin and tonic with her, she'd got a bit tipsy, and, well . . .

'Alex, do you mean he made a pass at you?'

She gave a half-laugh.

'I wonder why people say that, "made a pass", like in football? Well, if anybody made a pass, it was me, and the thing was, he totally failed to take the ball . . . He put down his G and T with a clang, like a garage door banging shut, and he instantly started talking about Derek, whom he'd never met, but whose mere existence was apparently enough to put him off . . . Lord, I was so embarrassed . . . Anyway, he made it fairly obvious that he didn't actually fancy me . . . If anything, I think you're more his type.'

'For goodness sake, Alex, let's keep me out of this!'

So much talk – I remember May as the month when we talked endlessly. Me and Sandra. Alexandra and I. Amazing to think that, at one point, I'd thought she was going to extract all my secrets and give me back nothing in return. Now it was the opposite. She talked endlessly about her life, about the big, glittery occasions, the charity fashion shows, the dinner dances she went to with Derek and his colleagues, and the get-togethers in Donegal at Hallowe'en and Easter, where a dozen of them and their kids would practically book the hotel out solid, and when the kids were in bed, they would be laughing and joking and carrying on in the bar till two AM, and how she amazed them all by being up at eight, when barely any of them were stirring, to go to the gym before breakfast . . .

'Do they still go to bed?' I asked.

'How d'you mean?'

'The kids, I mean, Denzil's nearly ten, and your others, they're practically adults. Do they still go to bed before you?'

'Oh, they watch DVDs. Used to.' She sighed. 'It's true, we haven't done Donegal for a while – I guess that's why I was so keen on the skiing in Andorra. That's one thing we can still do together.'

And then she talked more about how Derek couldn't do without her. He really couldn't. They did so much entertaining, and of course he left the entire running of the house to her, not to mention trying to keep poor wee Denzil on track, and no way were they going to end up living out that awful old movie cliché situation, where distinguished but weary middle-aged man heartlessly dumps devoted wife for younger, more glamorous model. No way. No one could be more glamorous than her and, what's more, nobody could be more organised.

She came out with a whole welter of stuff about how she was really, really important to Derek. But not much, I noticed, about whether Derek was really important to her. Not just as a distinguished consultant. But as a person. Was he giving her any emotional back-up at all? Was he giving her anything, apart from the status? Because she'd probably fall apart if she couldn't be Mrs Masterson. Oh, and the money, of course. That was pretty important.

Money was something she talked about a lot. She was amazed that, in the seven years since Rory and I had divorced, he had never upped what she called 'your maintenance', though it was Roisin's child support. I said my job was pretty well paid, I didn't need extra from Rory, we were managing fine, I'd rather not be beholden to Rory, actually. Besides, he had two wee kids and there was poor Denise having to keep up a full-time job, rushed off her feet.

She said, 'Well, whose idea was it for Rory and Denise to have two kids right away? All your idea, was it? Ha! They have two perfectly good salaries don't they? And they aren't having to struggle along without a car?

'You need a car, Vinny. You need to get him to up your child support in line with inflation, and then you can get a car. It's going to be really hard, doing without one, when Roisin's a teenager.'

Then she laughed and admitted, 'Sorry. I guess

this is just displacement activity. I know I should stop organising your life, and try to organise something for Denzil. Only I can't think what.'

We both went quiet.

Then she said, 'Last night we all had dinner together for once, and Denzil was telling us all about what he'd do with a gap year, when he was ten. And d'you know what Derek said afterwards?'

'Told Denzil to do two extra eleven-plus papers, to get all those silly ideas out of his head?'

'No. I mean, to me. What he said to me was, something like, maybe we should let Denzil have a year out, and stay at home and have intensive coaching for P6 English and Maths, then he wouldn't have to go to school and do all those time-wasting things like art and music and projects, he could just sharpen up his brains and do really well in the eleven-plus, after his extra year.'

'You're kidding!'

'No, he was. After I'd got all worked up, because among other things, there's no goddam way I'd give up my job and do childcare 24/7, though of course he doesn't actually know I've got a job, 'cause I keep conveniently forgetting to tell him – anyway – turns out he was— she put on an American accent—'*just being ironic*.'

'He doesn't seem the sort of person who'd do irony.'

'Not usually, at least he hasn't done, not for ages. That's one of the reasons why I think he might be seeing someone. He keeps getting these odd little frisky moments.'

Not long after this conversation, I actually saw her. The someone. At least that's what it looked like. It was one of those rare Friday afternoons when Roisin had gone home with a friend after school, and for once I didn't have a pile of marking to do. So I went to the pub after school with two colleagues, John and Alma. The pub was called the Pirate's Head, and it was one of those places that have little snugs in the back, where you can sit and have a quiet conversation. That's where I saw them – when I was on my way to the ladies. Derek was sitting and talking intensely to some woman, they were giving each other a hundred and one percent attention, and just as I paused to give a sideways glance and check if it was really him, he put his hand over hers and gave it a quick squeeze. It looked like she squeezed back, but it was hard to tell at that distance. The funny thing was, she didn't look younger or more glamorous than Alex; she actually looked to be in her late forties; she had that kind of salt-and-pepper hair meant to look distinguished and to camouflage any grey bits you might be starting to have. It was a bit overlong, looked like she needed a trip to the hairdresser's soon, and from what I saw of her face, she looked tired. It was a patient, humorous-looking face, but well-lived-in, a bit saggy. When I came back from the ladies, they were both gone. Had they seen me?

Of course I couldn't tell Alex. What was there to tell, anyway? That I saw Derek squeezing some woman's hand? She could have been a colleague, pouring out her professional problems, couldn't she . . . Alex was like a butterfly, darting vividly about, swooping down on one flower then off to the next; a fast, strong flying butterfly, the sort that actually migrate in winter instead of curling up on a windowsill and dying. She needed to keep moving steadily, to stay alive through the winter. If I told her something that would make her bright wings crumple and droop, or beat too frantically and use up all her energy, how would that help?

She had so much energy. She would chase the kids round the garden or bounce on the trampoline, showing off, showing she could do it as well as they could.

'You put me to shame,' I told her.

'Sure I do nothing, only stand around all day.'

'Working in a café? On your feet all the time?'

'Well, it's not very physical. I've given up the gym, the boredom of it was seeping into my brain. But it means I need to keep active. I still go jogging twice a day, of course.'

'You should have been a PE teacher.'

She flushed. 'Well, after the eleven-plus debacle, it was pretty obvious I wasn't going to be any kind of a teacher. Ever.'

Still, I thought. *Still. After all this time.*

Unity's sports day was at the end of May; Roisin was going home with a friend afterwards. Alex said she could easily arrange for Denzil to go home with a friend as well. And why didn't she pick me up after school and I could come and see her house, then everybody would be going home with a friend?

And so we drove up the Malone Road, and turned in at the gleaming black gates that swung open and closed smoothly behind us, untouched by human hand. And then we sat in her ominously glittering sun room. (Not a conservatory, she insisted. Conservatory sounds so old fashioned, like the small ads in the back of the *Radio Times*. Sounds like we're elderly.) It was all glass, a gleaming construction with a roof of swirling lines that seemed to soar upwards and meet at a slightly off-centre point, with no visible means of support.

Even the strategically placed coffee tables were glass. Though, mercifully, not the chairs. I'd been on my feet all day, putting out stuff for the obstacle races and umpiring games of UniHoc and Benchball. I sank gratefully into a wicker chair with soft green cushions, and waited for the shiny coffee machine to stop making growly noises and deliver.

'It's spectacular,' I said. 'How d'you keep it like this? All my windows are forever wanting cleaning, and they never seem to get it.'

'Oh, we have an army of cleaners,' she said.

'Twice a week everything's scrubbed within an inch of its life, and you wouldn't dare leave anything lying around. I mean, it's good for the kids to be tidy, but sometimes I just long to drop a few crumbs out here and then leave the patio doors open and invite a few birds in, to mess the place up.'

She went over to get the coffee. On the glass table beside me was a pile of glossy magazines, and a big round bowl made of expensive-looking smokey glass with a pattern of thin gold lines. It was full of those marble eggs, or agate or whatever that swirly semi-precious stuff is. I turned one over in my hand. It felt heavy and cool. I opened one of the magazines, *Northern Irish Interiors*, and there it was in all its glory: 'A Country House in the Heart of the City'. Photos of the house's tasteful interiors, and the long sweep of the lawn, piercingly green, with its carefully placed heathers and conifers, and also what we weren't seeing: the rose garden, which was of course described as 'a riot of colour'. By now, Alex was reading over my shoulder.

'Riot, my arse!' she said. 'You've never seen colour so carefully controlled. Scarlet is allowed, yellow and white, but no purple, and definitely no pink. Derek can't stand pink. He says it gives him indigestion.'

She said there was no point going round to look for roses that weren't out yet, but would I like a tour of the house?

'Maybe next time,' I said. 'Not today, my feet are killing me. I was just wondering, where in all this glassy glory do you put Denzil?'

'Oh, he doesn't come in here. God forbid he might touch one of the walls and leave – ew! – fingerprints. Derek comes here when he's tired out after work, when he needs to relax. And he can't relax if there's anything untidy or messy. He's always been a bit OCD, it got worse after he became a consultant . . . No, there's a wee lawn out the back where Stewart used to kick a ball, and Denzil has it now. It doesn't matter if the grass round there gets all scruffy and baldy.' She sighed. 'Still, you can see why he likes your garden, can't you? A bit less space, but a *lot* more scope. Sometimes I have this fantasy about borrowing a wee bit of your wilderness, you know, sneaking a few buttercups into the front lawn or a bit of bramble into the herbaceous border, seeing how long it would be before Derek would notice.'

I said that we really needed to talk about Denzil and couldn't keep putting it off. She sighed again. 'Alright, let's stop pretending it's a coffee morning, and we'll have a G and T, OK?'

There was a glass drinks cabinet behind a lush display of ferns. It was years since I'd inhaled the slightly bitter, unnerving scent of gin. The bubbles of the tonic burst with tiny explosions at the back of my throat, and I could feel a blessed coolness seeping right down to my hot, squashed feet. I took off my trainers and wiggled my toes gratefully.

'So how long have you lived here?'

'Oh, about five years . . . we started off in quite a small place. We traded up twice, we just seemed to need more and more space, or at least, Derek did . . . Imagine. My sister up in Portrush, she moved into a ramshackle cottage with a glorious view when she was a student, at Coleraine, and she's been there ever since . . . they did an extension but she says there simply isn't *time* to do house-hunting . . . Derek just can't understand how she's been in the same house for sixteen years. He thinks not 'trading up' is somehow on a par with being feckless and irresponsible.'

The heat was building up under the glass. Alex knocked back her gin and poured herself another one. 'You know what I used to call this place, when we first got it? The Crystal Palace. Like that big place they had in Victorian times, in London, on top of a hill . . . '

'That's right,' I said, 'it was built for the Great Exhibition, eighteen-fifty-something. But didn't it burn down?'

'Yes. I saw a TV programme about it. Imagine what it must have been like – all that glass glittering in the sunshine – and then the fire. How can glass and metal frames actually *burn*? The heat must have been intense. And so bright. Brighter than all the Eleventh Night bonfires put together. I bet you could see it all over London.'

'Well, don't try it,' I advised.

'Oh, I'm sure this glass doesn't burn, anyway. It's probably scientifically fireproofed in some obscure modern way. But you know, on winter nights when it's all bleak outside, I sometimes sit here and imagine the flames. The heat building up, getting fiercer and fiercer. The roaring—'

'Alex, does it ever occur to you that you need to get out more?'

'Ha. Well, that's the whole point of Lunch at Louisa's. Plenty of chat. Keeps your mind off things.'

I pressed the cool glass of gin against my forehead and said it really was getting awful hot, and could we open some windows? Alex keyed some numbers into a little pad beside the drinks cabinet. Nothing happened. She keyed in the numbers more slowly. Still nothing.

'Can't you just do it by hand?'

'No, it's all centrally controlled – damn system's on the blink again.'

'Well don't worry, maybe we could go out and sit on the lawn.'

'Not unless you want to get soaked,' she said. 'The sprinklers come on at six, they're on a time switch, and no, before you ask, I can't control them by hand either.'

'If it's nearly six, I should be going soon – and we still haven't talked about Denzil—'

She led me into the sitting room. Squashy leather sofa and armchairs; I felt my sweaty bare legs sticking to the leather. And cream-coloured. I couldn't believe children had ever lived there. She said, 'You know, I will make us some coffee after all, I've just realised if I have any more gin, there's no way I'd be able to drive you home—'
She clattered off into the kitchen, refusing my offers of help.

'No, you look knackered, you just stay right here and have a wee doze on the sofa.'

I stretched out my legs, away from the clammy leather, paddled my feet into the furry cream-coloured rug and yawned. It wasn't just my feet that were tired, it was my brain; we'd just had a staff meeting – over lunchtime on sports day, for goodness sake! – about the Key Stage two results being slightly down over last year, and should we be worrying about this, or had our results actually been skewed by the late arrival of the Patel twins from Pakistan, and although their English wasn't bad, had it been a mistake to let them sit the test when they'd only been in the school a month, and me feeling dreadfully responsible because I was the one who said, 'Ah sure, let them go ahead if they're so keen to do it' . . .

Just for a mad little errant moment, I pictured

Derek sitting out in the sun room with his G and T, and the low winter sun flashing on the extravagantly curved glass roof. And feeling utterly ground down by all his responsibilities and the NHS targets and waiting lists and operations being cancelled because anesthetists don't turn up – stuff I could barely imagine – and taking pleasure in the glacial simplicity of his glass palace, its clean lines keeping at bay all that messy, exhausting stuff about human beings and their bolshieness and inadequacy and unpredictability. Maybe he didn't care whether she was glamorous or not, maybe he just wanted her to listen – and it was too long since she'd been nursing, struggling with that sort of stuff on a daily basis, and she could no longer empathise.

I pulled myself together. I couldn't let myself think like this. I was her friend, and that wasmaking her so happy, it wasn't for me to start undermining it by trying to imagine what went on in her stiff, awkward husband's head, and whether it was ever anything like what went on in mine. So I stared round the room and concentrated on the photos: Derek receiving some sort of award, shaking hands with some bigwig, Stewart and Chloe and Denzil in their old primary school uniforms, a family shot of the three kids grinning sharply and the background fading into soft focus all around them. None of Alex, to my surprise.

When she came in with the coffee, I said 'Look,

I honestly feel like I'm tutoring your wee fella under false pretences. If he had another year . . . got a bit more mature . . . it's not that he's stupid. It's just he can't get his head round it. If I give him really hard stuff, like some of the maths, I can see him just curl up and play dead. Like one of those caterpillars, you know, the brown furry ones you get in the dunes, at the seaside? You pick it up and it thinks you're a predator and it just curls up and freezes till you put it back in the undergrowth. And why wouldn't he? Some of that maths is first-year grammar school stuff, it's not even in the P7 syllabus – let alone the P6. I can't give him these advanced concepts when he keeps forgetting even the basic ones . . . '

I took a deep breath.

'If he does this in November, the most he's going to get is the current equivalent of a C. Quite possibly a D.'

'I know,' she said. We looked at each other.

'So,' I went on, 'I shouldn't really be taking your money—'

'But what happens if you stop?' she said. 'Derek's going to insist we get another tutor. More grief. And Denzil *likes* coming to see you. The kids are happy, Derek's happy, we're happy. Aren't we?'

'OK,' I said. 'It's a rickety structure, but I won't burn it down.'

She stepped over and gave me a hug. 'Oh, and

another thing, Denzil says to tell you to tell Roisin that he's *really sorry* she can't come to his birthday party.'

'Oh, when is it?'

'First of June. Next Saturday. Double figures at last. I thought he could have a day off coaching.'

'First of June? Maybe she could—'

'No, the thing is, he can't invite her. Because it's all boys. They're doing a sort of junior paintballing. Can you imagine, ten sweaty wee boys and your Roisin – wouldn't work, would it?'

I agreed that it wouldn't. I could see that Roisin would feel completely out of it. Scornful and suspicious – that's pretty much how boys and girls feel about each other, at this age. And Denzil would never be able to live down the embarrassment of having invited a girl to his birthday, a girl who wasn't even a sister or a cousin.

'Will she mind?' Alex asked.

'Maybe a bit. But it's all part of growing up, isn't it?'

'Oh Lord, growing up. Let's not go there.'

I turned the empty coffee mug round and round in my hands. 'No. Let's not.'

In the car, as she was driving me home, she said 'You should give a party, Vinny.'

I explained, 'Roisin has one every year, in fact, she's going to be eleven at the beginning of July, and—'

'No, Vinny, I meant a party for you.'

'For me?'

'Yes, a grown-up party. Invite the neighbours, some of your colleagues . . . and you could invite Chris.'

'Chris?'

'You know. The flag man. The veg man.'

'Lord, I'd forgotten his name. Why on earth should I invite him?'

'He definitely fancies you. When I . . . all that stuff about Derek. It wasn't the thought of Derek put him off, at all. It's just I'm really not his type. He needs someone a bit more sort of . . . quiet, and thoughtful. And deep. Like you.'

I laughed it off, told her I only appeared quiet and deep because my energy levels were pretty much at rock bottom. The picture of Alex trying to get off with Chris was so embarrassing, so appalling, I just pushed the whole thing as far away into the back of my mind as I possibly could.

The next day was Saturday; when Alex dropped Denzil off for his session, she said briskly 'I'll just pop upstairs and say hi to Roisin.'

'I'm not sure if this is a good moment—'

Roisin had been grumpy since she came back from Crystal's house. They'd been watching all kinds of rubbish on Crystal's new iPad that she got for her birthday; it was a proper iPad, and Crystal was quite happy to tell everybody that it cost £400.

She was shocked to hear that Roisin didn't have a laptop or tablet at all, that she just had to make do with the same boring old computer that her mum did all her teaching stuff on. It was just *so* not cool. So what did Roisin do? Only turn round and say she'd be getting exactly the same model for her birthday.

That wasn't like Roisin. Normally she's sensible to the point of being unnaturally cautious, for a ten-year-old. It's how I realised this new friendship with Crystal was on fairly rocky foundations, because in order to impress her, she had to come out with some fairly un-Roisinlike stuff. So I tried to explain to Roisin that if she got a tablet for her birthday, it would have to be the cheapest we could get, from Tesco's maybe, because we were going to Canada and had to save up. She said this wasn't fair, her dad and Denise and Saoirse and Fiona were going to Spain, and they didn't have to save up. And I said, well, sometimes life isn't fair.

Alex came down the stairs and gave me a cheery wave on her way out. So I presumed she'd told Roisin about how Denzil was sorry he couldn't invite her to his party. And I presumed Roisin was OK about it. But it needled away at me, and all the time I was trying to stop Denzil's mind wandering, mine was actually wandering too. Wouldn't it have been better if Alex had said nothing, and just let sleeping dogs lie? But then, Denzil might have casually let slip something about it later on, and she might have been upset if she found out retrospectively that there'd been a party, and she hadn't been invited . . . Oh Lord, kids. I had them all day long, with their wee emotional outbursts and their inability to grasp even the basics of the adult world, and I had Roisin evenings and weekends, and now I had Denzil too, and what on earth was I going to do about him?

As soon as the session was over, he shouted cheerily upstairs, 'Are you coming out into the garden?'

I heard her muffled reply. Something about 'project work' and 'finish'. Denzil was clearly nonplussed. A few minutes later, he came back in, shouting up the stairs again 'Are you finished yet?' She replied 'Alright, alright, I'm coming' and eventually she appeared, looking a bit sulky. But by the time Alex came to pick Denzil up I could see them both bouncing on the trampoline, and they came in pink and out of breath, and beaming as usual.

'So that's all OK then?' Alex whispered to me as she shepherded Denzil out to the car.

'Guess so,' I whispered back.

But that evening I heard her talking on her mobile to one of her friends. 'I don't want to go to his stupid old birthday, anyway' and I felt my stomach give a lurch, but what could I say?

Sunday night she came back from her dad's in a total, state of whinge. 'Saoirse got one.'

'Got a what?'

'An iPad. For her birthday. For her *fourth* birthday. And I'm going to be eleven and I'm not even getting one for my eleventh.'

I heaved a mighty sigh. 'What on earth does she need an iPad for?'

'You can watch cartoons and you can do this great wee game – she showed me—'

I told her books were better for four year olds. Being read to. Talking. 'Screens at that age aren't good, you know, research has shown, it doesn't help their wee brains develop—'

Then on Tuesday, things boiled over. Denzil came in, crestfallen, because they'd started giving out actual marks for the tests at school. Up to now, they'd only marked sections, but now he was faced with the enormity of always getting at least five marks lower than anyone else in his class. He kept gazing out the window, which was pretty much his normal style, but all his answers were monosyllabic, which wasn't a bit like him. And Roisin was no help at all. Instead of joining him in the garden after the session she just kept hanging round me, whingeing. I was trying to get some marking done, thinking I'd have half an hour before Alex came to pick Denzil up, and the kids would be busy outside, but then there she was in the kitchen, getting in my hair.

'Why don't you go and play with Denzil?'

'I don't *play* with Denzil,' she said grandly.

'We design things.'

'Well, go and design some more of your assault course.'

'It's too difficult. There's a huge gap all along the back of the house, and we can't get across it. I wish we had a climbing frame. At dad's they have a climbing frame and it's got, like, a wee wooden castle on the top and a wavy slide coming down out of it. And Denise rigged up the paddling pool so they can come down the slide and land in the water. It's a bit too hard for Fiona because she's only just three and she doesn't really like the wavy slide but Saoirse loves coming down it and having a really big splash. I wish *we* had a paddling pool.'

'Roisin, you *had* a paddling pool! You grew out of it by the time you were seven, you said it was babyish!'

'Well, I wasn't making an assault course then, was I?'

She glared at me. Sometimes Roisin actually looks quite sweet when she's sulking, but this time there was a fierce hostile little accuser I'd never seen before, glaring out of her hazel eyes. That were so like Rory's.

So when she said, 'And if it's wet they can go to the swimming pool or Adventure Land, they don't have to wait for buses, they can go in the car, my dad takes them everywhere in the car—' something snapped in me, and I heard myself saying,

'Well maybe you should bloody go and live at your dad's then!'

Roisin turned red, bust into tears, rushed up the stairs.

In the silence that filled the kitchen, I heard a voice say 'Ouch.'

It was Alex, standing in the doorway. She must have let herself in. I flopped onto one of the hard angular kitchen chairs, put my head down melodramatically on a pile of marking.

'Oh my God, I can't believe I said that, of course I didn't mean it, will she think I meant it?'

'Go after her,' Alex said. 'Then she'll probably scream at you. Say you're sorry. Then you can leave her for up to an hour. You've got about an hour to think of how you're going to explain yourself before she starts to bury the thing and goes all brittle and can't talk about it.'

'How come you know so much about it?'

She laughed.

'I've had three. I've screamed at all of them. Then tip-toed around trying to soothe their hurt feelings. You get better at it. You also get more tired, of course. Sometimes you get so tired you can barely open your mouth, but yes, you do get better at it.'

I crept upstairs and found Roisin lying all curled up under her duvet. I patted the bumpy bit that was probably her shoulder, and said 'Sweetheart, I am *so* sorry. I totally didn't mean that, I promise.'

She just squirmed away. I crept back downstairs again.

'Well, there's no sign of her being brittle yet. In fact there's no sign of her at all, just a bunched-up duvet that isn't speaking to anyone.'

Alex laughed and handed me a mug of coffee. It was too hot, and not like I usually make it myself, there was a kind of sweetness I didn't recognise.

'Did you put sugar in this?'

'Vanilla essence.'

'I didn't know I had any.'

'Well, you do. I found it at the back of the top shelf of a cupboard.'

I sighed. 'What am I going to do with her?'

'Oh, she'll be fine. You just drop all that marking for half an hour and give her a bit of quality time, watch some rubbish TV or do some baking with her.'

Alex took the mug back from me, shook out a few drops from an ancient bottle of chocolate essence which must have been in the cupboard since I'd moved in, sprinkled a bit of cinnamon on top and handed it back to me.

'Thing is, it's maybe time you worked through your anger about Rory.'

I protested that I didn't have any anger, it was a perfectly civilised parting, the thing just fizzled out and we both moved on, we were still friends . . .

'He was your teenage romance wasn't he?' she said. 'So you want to hang on to the memories. You want to keep the illusion intact. You don't want to spoil it by asking him for more money for Roisin, or giving out to him about not taking Roisin on holiday, and even forgetting to pick her up. You don't know how he'd react to that. So who do you get cross with? Roisin.'

'Whoa,' I said. 'Teenage romance? I was twenty-two when we met.'

'Aye but you were such a good wee girl, all hard-working and conscientious and buttoned up, you probably wouldn't let yourself unbutton till you were twenty-two, and then of course you picked someone wildly unsuitable and got swept off your feet—'

'Oh yeah!' I said. 'Like you know how to pick them!'

She said in a broad Belfast accent, '*Watch your mouth wee girl*' and we laughed, and hugged each other. She said she was taking Denzil away so I could have some quiet time to mend fences with Roisin, and would I think about that other stuff? I said maybe, and goodbye to Denzil, wished him a great birthday party and I went upstairs to mend fences with Roisin.

I opened the door of her room quietly, so she didn't hear me.

All my old Barbies and all her old Barbies were strutting about, trying on each other's clothes, posing in the mirror, laughing and having a good old gossip. At least that, for a stunned moment, is what it looked like.

Of course it was actually Roisin doing the talking and making them stride about; organising this event, just as she would one day organise a bunch of real people, because this child was going to be an organiser one day, no doubt about it. And blessed are those who can forget their broken hearts by throwing themselves into organising something.

I closed the door silently. Only a few more months for imaginative play to run its course: usually by the time the child's eleven, or soon after, that's pretty much over forever. I could feel time running out for her.

Ten minutes later I went upstairs again, knocked loudly this time, told her again that I honestly didn't mean it, I only said it because I was tired and cross, and did she want to watch TV with me or make something? She said make something and, in fact, there was a packet of chocolate fairy cake mix complete with icing. It emerged from the same back of the top shelf place that Alex had been rootling around in.

So we made fairy cakes, and a list. I remembered what Alex said about having a party and I thought, *What the heck, Denzil's having a party and not inviting Roisin, Roisin's having a party in July and of course won't invite Denzil, why don't I have a party in between and I can just invite everybody I know*? It wouldn't be that many, really, and I didn't even have to worry about the grass getting trampled to mud or the patio doors getting smeared by sticky fingers or the carpet getting drink spilt on it, because, unlike the Mastertons' Crystal Palace, my home is already a tip, and there's nothing well-groomed or shiny to smear or spoil.

'Can I invite a friend?' Roisin asked.

'We could be waitresses.'

'Waitresses?'

It turned out she envisaged not herself and the supercilious Crystal, I was glad to hear, but herself and the much more down-to-earth Zoe, carrying trays of little canapés and offering them to the grown-ups. This would include teachers from Unity, but that didn't faze her as she liked all her teachers.

'Anyhow,' she commented cheerily, 'practically everyone you know is a teacher.' She thought for a bit, then added 'Will you be inviting the veg man?'

'The veg man? Why?'

'Well, he's quite fun really. Also the good thing about him is that he isn't a teacher.'

She helped me draft an email inviting everyone to a summer garden party, with a photo of an actual foxglove growing in our garden. Foxgloves seed themselves: they don't need any attention, and they're about the only thing I can grow successfully.

I dashed it off to practically everyone I knew, while Roisin busied herself with little drawings of the canapés she and Zoe were going to make. Little shrimps on cucumber slices on round crackers. Tangerine segments on cream cheese on round crackers. All her canapés were round, like stickers of smiley faces.

The slight problem with inviting the veg man was that I didn't know his email address. Alex kept texting me to say how exited she was about the party, it was about time I did something for myself, and had I invited Chris yet? What was the problem? Surely I didn't need his email address, didn't I see him every week?

So the next time he came, there I was, practically lying in wait, and then it just all seemed so false, I couldn't bring myself to raise the subject. For once he didn't hang about on the doorstep, he was through into my messy kitchen in a trice, with the door shut behind him.

'Thing is,' he said, 'I don't think anyone saw me taking down that flag. And if they did, it's OK, they don't know where I live. But if they did see me, and then they saw me again with the van, then that puts the van at risk. The van could get attacked just driving through a Loyalist area.'

I sighed. 'I never thought of that. I shouldn't have made you take that flag down.'

'You didn't make me. I hate this coat-trailing as

much as you do. Each new flag a new little snarl of aggression. Anyhow, the great thing is, they haven't put up another one. I doubt if I could repeat that performance.'

'You deserve a medal,' I said. 'Have a coffee and half a scone.'

As we crossed the straggly lawn to the stone terrace, he suddenly clapped his hands and started shouting. Something black and white streaked across in front of us, almost tripping us up, and hurled itself up into the old rhododendron where it crouched on a thick branch, glaring at us.

'*Bad* cat,' he said firmly.

The air was full of indignant churring sounds. On the grass, just a foot away from the shelter of the ivy wreathing the dead rowan tree, were two minute brown bundles. Ever-so-slightly fuzzy. Crouching with their tiny wings spread pleadingly, they ignored us and kept up a constant high-pitched tseeptseeptseep . . . a tiny sound that stopped abruptly when another little brown bird, without the fuzz, landed beside them and stuffed something microscopic and grey and wriggling into their gaping beaks.

'Wrens,' he exclaimed, delighted. 'You've got wrens nesting in your ivy.'

'In there? In the dead rowan tree?'

'You'd be surprised what could be in there,' he said. 'When did it die?'

'Four years ago. All of a sudden. I remember exactly when it was, because we had a visiting poet in the school, doing workshops, and I got a bit carried away and wrote a poem myself. About the tree.'

'That's pretty impressive,' he said. 'I've never managed more than a few muttered curses when stuff of mine dies. Do you still have it?'

While I was making the coffee, I found it in a kitchen drawer along with some of Roisin's drawings that were so good I wanted to keep them. When I came back out to the garden, I handed him the poem wordlessly.

It's as if my favourite tree
Has committed suicide.
Now all I can see from my window
Are buds that opened, then shrivelled,
Concrete-grey branches
Poking at the sky
Like an awkward modern sculpture.
Come, bramble and ivy,
Wrap it in soft green,
Make it bristle with blossoms,
A dream of jungles out there
For me to gaze upon.

He squinted at the tree.

'I see what you mean about the modern sculpture,' he said. 'And now you've got your jungles, too. There's no telling what might be nesting in there.'

I rambled on about how I'd always been meaning to get it cut down, but it's so hard to get round to things, and now I was kind of glad I'd left it . . . the same applied to most of the garden.

He looked pointedly at the huge, straggly rhododendron.

'Well, that's a bit far gone. You might as well grub that out completely and start again; nothing ever grows under or around *rhododendron ponticum*. You see the skill is, with a garden, knowing what to take out, and what to cut back, and what to just leave.

'You'd think, once something dies, that's the end, wouldn't you? But leaving the rowan tree was a good thing, environmentally. It's probably hosting masses of wildlife. You have to know when to interfere, and when to leave things to develop in their own time.'

'So you don't think it's all just a total shambles?'

'Well, it's never going to win any prizes for the best-kept garden, but life is about more than just competitions, isn't it?'

I sighed.

'Some people don't think so.' It was only when he got up to leave, that I realised I hadn't invited him. Quickly, before we got to the doorstep, I gabbled, 'OhbythewayI'mhavingapartySaturdaythirteenthJunesevenishwouldyouliketocome?'

He looked embarrassed; his face, always brown and weatherbeaten, now seemed to have gone all red under the brown.

'Oh. Should I bring my partner?'

'Partner?'

'Renata. Renata Keller. She's—' he took a breath '—my business partner and my domestic partner. Like she always says.'

'Where is she from?' I asked stupidly.

'Dusseldorf.'

We stared at each other.

'Yeah – sure – of course—' I stammered. I must have gone even redder than he had. 'So now you'd better get back into the van quick – before anyone sees you—'

And I practically slammed the door in the poor man's face.

Goddammit, I thought, I could have sworn, if ever I saw a single guy hanging around with one arm longer than the other, this is the one. And I got it totally, completely wrong. And so, I realised, did Alex. She'd tried to get off with him – how come she hadn't realised – I felt like texting her, just to say –

To say what, exactly? What was the problem? He was just a perfectly pleasant, friendly guy. To try and make something else out of the whole thing would be like that protracted and in retrospect really rather cringe-making episode when we were in P6, when we both decided that awkward, angular Miss Chisolm, who taught P7, needed a boyfriend; we spent many happy, fruitless hours plotting how to get her hooked up with some poor chap, the visiting minister, the one unmarried male teacher in the school, even the caretaker.

No, I decided. I'd be saying nothing to Alex. There'd been too much said already, too much about all sorts of things, I was getting too dependent on her, it was time I created a bit of space round myself. Got my sense of proportion back. Got my life into some sort of order. Stood on my own two feet.

And I fiercely began to grub up the weeds from between the ancient cracked paving stones on the terrace. The woman I'd bought the house from, Mrs Marshall, had lived there on her own. She was in her eighties, and I remember her apologising for those weeds, saying she didn't have the strength in her hands any more, and the first summer I had the house, I used to come out here and religiously pull them all up, as if I was somehow helping out an old lady.

But a few weeks later they'd be back, little ragged green and white things. Some had microscopic pink flowers, and then there'd be pale ethereal seedy things that looked like the wings of dead moths, after a cat's been at them and they get all shredded. Those weeds, or their ancestors, went back a long way, maybe back to when the terrace was first constructed, or thrown together, in the nineteen fifties or maybe even the nineteen thirties? So after a while, I just left them to it.

But now there was going to be a party, an event that I'd envisaged as a refreshing thing, like a trickle of spring water, but it had turned into an ominously spreading puddle, like when you realise, with a sickening feeling, that you filled your washing machine too full, and now it's determined to overflow. I kept getting texts and emails and even the odd phone call:

—Should I bring something?

—Is it your birthday?

—Is it OK if we bring our baby, he'll probably sleep most of the time, can we park him somewhere out of the way?

There were going to be thirty people, maybe even forty, trampling about in the garden, with its odd collection of hardware deposited by Roisin and Denzil. They would stand on my terrace, dipping their plastic cups into a big bowl of summer punch on the plastic table, and round their feet would be a smooth expanse of paving, all weeded out by hand, no nasty toxic weedkillers poisoning the bugs and the caterpillars. Anyway, I couldn't afford weedkiller.

So I weeded and weeded, and when my nails were all caked with earth and my back stiff and my knees sore, I heated up frozen pizzas for me and Roisin and scolded her off to bed and ran a bath without putting the light on, so that I could just lie there and gaze at the square of sky framed in my bathroom window, as it gradually turned a deeper and deeper blue, then finally a wistful, sulky sort of navy. And that was the last day of May over.

I crawled out of my cold bath, and for once managed not to text Alex, and went to bed.

JUNE

Denzil was beaming when he came for the next session. I asked him how the party was, and was it nice being ten at last, but it turned out all he wanted to talk about was his essay.

'Essay?' I asked.

Yes; Mrs Moncrieff had told them, with all these eleven-plus papers, it was about time they did something else to get a bit of balance, and when they got to big school they would have to write lots of essays, so she would let them be very grown-up and choose from a choice of three titles, and Denzil had chosen 'My Ideal Home'.

'And it was great!' he said. 'I got an A! And my mum says I can show it to you, but it has to stay in my school bag till after the session.'

I could practically see it burning a hole in his schoolbag, the way money is supposed to burn a hole in kids' pockets. He was fairly jumping with excitement; his eyes didn't glaze over after the first five minutes, as they usually did – it took a full forty-five minutes for that to happen. Even when he got muddled, for the eleventeenth time, over converting grammes to kilos (divide by a thousand) and converting metres to centimeters (divide by a hundred), he wasn't as depressed as usual. More like indignant.

'It's daft!' he complained. 'Why do they keep saying metres one minute and centimetres the next, why don't they just have everything in metres, then there wouldn't be anything to trip you up?'

'Denzil, they're trying to trip you up, they want to know if you know how to convert . . . '

He was crestfallen again. But not for long. As soon as the session was over, he flourished the essay and insisted that I first read Mrs Moncrieff's comment: 'Very well expressed, Denzil, and your spelling is impeccable.'

'Roisin helped me, but mostly just with the spelling,' he asserted proudly.

How had Roisin helped him? I asked. Because surely they hadn't seen each other for a week? Oh, he said, he'd sent it to her as a Skype message, then they'd talked about it on Skype . . .

'Since when is Roisin on Skype?'

He beamed. 'I helped her set it up. My mum says I'm more technically savvy than she is.'

'They're both geniuses.' Alex's cheery voice came from the doorway. 'Scarper, Denzil, I want to talk to Vinny.'

She made the coffee, while I read the essay. It was rather poignant. Denzil's 'Ideal Home' bore a strange resemblance to my pokey, run-down little house. It seemed he really liked the pillars holding up the ceiling, and the way you could stick things on them with Blu-Tack, and the way the downstairs was nearly all one big room, sort of friendly and cosy. And he liked the history, the fact that it was built for a soldier who'd come back from the First World War, and if he was still feeling a bit shell-shocked, the soldier could look out of the upstairs window and see the trees at the back, all green and peaceful.

But most of all, he liked the garden, because there were loads of bushes and it was the best place he knew for hide and seek and climbing trees and he and his friend were making a brilliant assault course and it was going to be called Wilderness Land, and when it was finished they might even be able to charge admission, because his friend could do with a bit more pocket money.

'Did you notice how it's all in paragraphs?' Alex asked. 'That's Roisin's doing. She eased him into the paragraphs so subtly, he didn't even realise she was doing it. That is one very, very smart girl you have.'

'Yeah, I don't have to worry about her, thank goodness.'

'Are you sure ? I mean, there's worries and there's worries. Are you sure you're doing the right thing, not sending her to grammar school? Because she's a born teacher, isn't she?'

I said sharply that Unity was an all-ability school.

'It's not like Rushfield, particularly Rushfield in the bad old days. To put it crudely, it's got a bottom and a middle and a top.'

'Yeah,' she said. 'Rushfield didn't even have a middle, did it? I can see that Unity would have a very happy middle, no pressure, like, but how do you get the top kids? Don't the parents want them to go to grammar school?'

I tried to explain the seething mass of motives: the impeccable and the not-so-impeccable; Group One idealists, who think integrated education is the only way our wee country can break out of its sectarian straitjacket and move forward; Group Two idealists, who think their kids are so bright, it'd be good for them to rub up against less able kids, because that's who they're going to have to work with when they're grown up; Group One pragmatists, the ones with mixed marriages who don't want their kids to be sniped at and sneered at by either side; Group Two pragmatists, who can't be bothered with the whole transfer test charade and just think, what the hell, if I can just get the eldest into Unity then the other two can go as a matter of course, and nobody has to go through all that ghastly coaching and box-ticking and sore-tummy-because-of-nerves business.

'Personally,' I went on, 'I probably come into all four of those groups, and maybe a couple of others as well.'

'Wow,' Alex commented, 'that's quite a speech. Pity Derek wasn't here to listen to it. Because in some ways, it sounds like Unity might suit Denzil better than the grammar schools, which he isn't going to get into anyway, but it's no use telling that to Derek – he's neither an idealist nor a pragmatist, he's some kind of third group, a totally-set-in-his-ways-ist—'

Denzil and Roisin burst in just as I was starting to explain that Roisin would get into Unity, no problem, being at an integrated primary school plus being an eldest-or-only child, but Denzil, with two older siblings at grammar schools, that would be a different story . . .

I don't think she even heard me. She was busy scolding Denzil and pretending to cuff him. 'Mrs Corcoran loved your essay, pet, but she doesn't love your muddy shoes on her kitchen floor.'

I said that it didn't matter, and of course I loved his essay, and I asked him what made him call that thing out there Wilderness Land? Roisin answered for him: 'Well, you always say it's a wilderness and the veg man says it's a wilderness and even Denzil's dad. But it has to be Wilderness Land, because, you know, there's Indiana Land, Adventure Land, Dinosaur Land'

'Look, we rigged up a rope in the big apple tree,' Denzil exulted, 'and now we can swing down onto the trampoline, and then there's only a bit left, just across the back of the house, before we get on to the car port roof, and I was thinking . . . ' he put on his I'm-so-cute-and-sort-of-goofy-how-could-you-bear-to-deny-me-anything expression, which I'd seen him use a couple of times with his mum, obviously never with me. 'If I could get up the roof on a ladder, and tie a rope round the chimney—'

'No way!' Alex and I simultaneously.

'Oh. Well anyway, do you want to come and watch us doing it, I mean, doing it as far as we've got?'

I looked at my watch.

'Honestly Denzil I'd love to, but I've got all these school reports . . . '

'On Saturday,' said Alex firmly. 'I'll bring some lunch, and we'll both watch you doing the whole thing from beginning to end.'

'Promise?' Roisin asked.

'Promise,' Alex said, and she dragged Denzil away, calling from the doorstep 'I'll text you, we should talk about me bringing food for the party, maybe I'll even send you an email and you can read it when you have a wee gap in your hectic schedule—'

Why was I giving a party at one of the busiest times of the year, with thirty-odd school reports to churn out and thirty-odd parents to have in-depth sessions with over successive afternoons and evenings? Why put more pressure on myself? And what was I going to say to Johnny's parents? They were wondering, as was I, whether he should give up the coaching, because it was probably hopeless. But on the other hand, he didn't seem to mind the sessions, and I was embarrassingly, shamingly reluctant to give up the £50 a week? And what about Denzil? It was getting clearer and clearer that he hadn't a bat's chance in hell of getting into grammar school, unless maybe he could repeat P6, it wasn't entirely unheard of . But then what if he repeated the year and still didn't get into grammar school, wouldn't his wee ego be in shreds?

Roisin went off upstairs to skype Zoe, whom she hadn't seen for at least two hours, to discuss their waitress costumes. Roisin would be fine. Roisin would always be fine. Of course she didn't want to go to grammar school – why should she – just to prove she could?

I took my pile of reports to the garden, humping them up the steps of the terrace – still a few weeds, which I hadn't dealt with, on those steps – and installing myself at the plastic table. It was a heavy, sultry evening. I tried to ignore the jumble of ropes stretched around me, and concentrate. But there was all this sort of high-pitched, distant screaming. Whose kids could possibly be making a noise like that? I leaned back, gazed up at the grey curdled sky, listened. Way, way above me, something tiny and black soared and swooped and came back, then a couple of others, then there were half a dozen of them screaming their heads off. Swifts.

I remembered what Chris had said, that there'd be gangs of teenage swifts roaming the skies soon. When was that? Must be several weeks since we'd had that conversation in the street with him, when Roisin asked were they swallows, and he said no they were swifts, fathers feeding their young. In that time, the young had grown from helpless babies to great big noisy bruisers.

I gave up. There was just no way I could concentrate. I'd done nineteen, and there were only another eleven to do, and if I set my alarm for an hour earlier in the morning I could get loads done before school. I gorged on pancakes with Roisin, then after I'd nagged her off to bed I ran a bath and just lay there, in clouds of steam, gazing vacantly up at the window. There must have been a sunset outside, brash and vivid, but only its feeble afterglow reached into the bathroom. I lay there and tried to empty my mind.

Denzil kept popping back into it. And Roisin. And even Chloe, with her borrowed ID and her pained, exasperated father. When we were young, I thought, there was none of this, no going out at night, it wasn't safe, so things are better for kids nowadays . . . aren't they? And now they're writing books about the Troubles, and making films, it's all getting talked about and analysed and chewed over . . . but this other stuff. That doesn't get talked about. Nobody writes books about parents who agonise and spend thousands on coaching, and then the darn kid doesn't get into grammar school after all. Nobody makes films about kids who fail to scrape into grammar school, do they? Unless of course the kids are out rioting. That still happens sometimes. And then they become visible, they become talked about.

A tiny fly was crawling up the damp window pane. Not really a fly – some kind of small, random insect with sickle-shaped wings. Its progress was impeded by the steam. Sometimes it seemed all scrunched up, no shape at all and hardly moving; other times it would break free, or hit a drier patch, and resume its arrowhead-shaped crawling. The wings made it look like a tiny swallow. Or more likely a swift: seen through the steam, it had no colour, it just looked black, or a kind of sooty dark grey. Swallows go on the ground sometimes, but apparently swifts never do.

I wrapped myself in a towel, and opened the window. If this wee fella could get away from the glassy desert of steam, he could presumably fly just as well as the next insect – if somebody didn't come along and crush him first.

It was still only seven thirty, and I was on my twenty-first report, when the doorbell rang. A woman I didn't recognise appeared, thin and wiry with a sun-tanned face and hair tied up in a scarf, she was wearing a striped shirt and dungarees. It was ages since I'd seen anyone in dungarees. She was carrying a box. Locally Organic.

'I am Renata. I brought your vegetables,' she said, in a voice with only a slight trace of an accent. 'Because today Chris couldn't come.'

I gazed at her and found myself asking dopily, 'Why?'

She shrugged. 'He is seeing his mother. She is old, and sick. Again.'

I went to take the box from her, assuming she'd go straight away, but she just stood there. Watching me.

'I have to take the box back,' she said firmly. 'He leaves them in people's houses, and then we have no boxes.'

I picked up a bag of onions and a couple of carrots, and stood there helplessly, as if I couldn't remember where they went.

She asked impatiently, 'You like me to put them away?'

'No, no, of course not – Well maybe just the tomatoes and celery, they go in the fridge—'

She put them away and then stood back, hands on hips, studying Roisin's drawings that were stuck up on the fridge with little magnets. An imaginary landscape: mountains, a waterfall. Two people paddling a canoe. A bear catching a salmon. There was a definite Canadian theme. And then a swallow, just like the one on the little necklace Alex had finally got after all those years. It gave me quite a start, seeing it four times bigger than life size, and with a curious sort of smiley expression on its face. How can a bird have a smile when it doesn't have a mouth, just a beak?

Renata said, 'Your child is very creative. In Irish schools there is not enough art, I think.'

'Oh no – I mean, that's true—'

She had a wrinkled red pepper in her hand, that must have come out of the fridge.

'This you need to throw in the compost.'

I found myself apologising – 'Oh, I'm afraid we don't have a compost bin, I'll just throw it in the rubbish—'

'You should have a compost heap,' she explained patiently, as if to a child.

'And you should plant vegetables. All this good land wasted, all bushes with no fruit—'

'Well,' I said, surprising myself, 'I'm planning to cut down that rhododendron. Then I'll be planting . . . courgettes. You come back next spring, you'll see.'

She shook her head.

'Next spring. No. I won't be here.'

'Oh?'

'Soon I am leaving. Back to Germany. I have a job. He doesn't know yet. About the job. But I think he knows anyway I will go, some time soon.'

I said stupidly, 'Is it because of all the sectarian stuff, and the flags and the racist attacks—'

'No. It is because Irish men spend too much time visiting their mothers. Also, the education system. This is not where I want to raise my child.'

I could feel myself blushing to the roots of my hair.

'He never mentioned you have a child—'
She laughed

'Not yet. But it's time. I will be thirty-five soon. If I had a child here, I would be sending it to the Steiner school. But Chris would not.

He says, 'Bad enough running a crank business, without being a crank parent as well'. So you see? Better I should go back and have a child in Germany. Where nobody has to start letters and numbers at four years old.'

I took the red pepper from her, flinching away so our hands didn't touch. She just stood there, looking at me appraisingly. I thought wildly: Is she trying to see if I'm suitable? A woman who wouldn't mind a man who visited his mother too much? She and Alex both, trying to get me off with someone who delivered veg round the doors . . . impossible.

She said 'Thank you for inviting me to your party. I will be happy to come.'

I bent down to put the desiccated red pepper in the bin, and when I straightened up, she was gone. There was just cold air where she'd been standing. As if I'd only imagined her, made up the sort of partner Chris would have, someone completely different from me. Someone with restless, efficient energy, who'd ruthlessly throw out shrivelled vegetables. Who'd firmly grasp at relationships, and get what she wanted; then calmly discard it, when it wasn't what she wanted any more.

She'd been there; the veg was the proof; she'd been in my kitchen less than ten minutes, and she'd left all this turmoil. And I had to get on with the wretched reports, but part of me was glad, part of me wanted even more reports to bury my nose in, so I wouldn't have to emerge and confront things. Roisin and Denzil and Alex and stroppy Derek and Chris with his 'Sometimes even now, I can feel my brothers breathing down my neck.' And all of them with feelings and moods that you had to tip-toe carefully round. And me, most of all, worn out with the strain of having to tiptoe carefully round myself.

On Saturday Alex brought Pyrex boxes full of little frozen pinwheels of bacon and mustard and leek and olive.

'I'll just pop these in your freezer,' she explained,

'and you take them out the night before the party, and there you are . . . trays of trouble-free stuff.'

'Trouble free', I said heavily.

'What?' she said.

I could feel the tightness in the back of my neck, as if my head couldn't dip and turn and stretch freely, as if it was clamped rigid to the top of my spine and there'd be an awful headache starting soon and I'd be wanting to snap at everybody. So I gave Denzil thirty minutes of timed English questions to do, and instructed Roisin to keep him at it, while working on her flags project. Alex and I were heading out, I said, to enjoy a wee bit of peace and quiet in the garden.

There'd been a day, I couldn't remember when exactly, when Alex and I had lain out in the sun, both of us glossy with Ambre Solaire, and played that old game we used to play at school, 'Where in the world would you most like to be at this moment?' Canada, I'd said, with snow on the peaks of the Rocky Mountains, real snow that never melts all year round, but hot hot sunshine too, and me going up in a cable car and getting out on a wooden landing stage and gazing down at the conifers and breathing in that lovely scent of pine trees – and Alex had interrupted and said I'd pinched her fantasy, only hers was in the Alps, with all that sun and scenery too but without the sweat of having to do impressive skiing and follow it up with impressive apres-skiing and then get up next morning and do yet more impressive skiing . . . and those pine trees I could smell were in Austria, not in Canada, and we'd ended up having a play fight, just like in P6, and stuffing grass down each other's necks.

Today the sun was shining, but this time there was definitely no scent of pine trees. Lying on the hard ground was making my head worse, not better, and Alex's eyes had a puffy, underslept look, and she positively reeked of Life is Beautiful, or whatever that thing was. I'd gradually come to realise that she tended to wear too much perfume when she was worried.

'Well,' she said, 'Derek talked Chloe out of the Gap Year idea. She's going straight to Queen's in September.'

'So that's good . . . isn't it?'

'Not entirely, no. He is now back to full-time micro-managing of Denzil's life. It's finally beginning to dawn on him that short of a brain transplant, nothing's going to get Denzil into grammar school.'

I took a deep breath.

'So that's . . . also good?'

'Not really. No. He's been asking around and making exhaustive searches on the Internet and you know what he came up with? Craigmillan.' Another deep breath. I knew Craigmillan of course, I'd been to a concert there once with Alma McCrory from Unity, well-groomed little boys in impeccable uniforms singing with well-groomed impeccability in a great soaring Gothic chapel in a lush woodland. It was cast in the mould of a minor English public school, but now it was taking in Cs and even Ds, so I'd heard; unlike Unity, it was struggling to keep up its numbers. Come to think of it, that must have been why we were there. I vaguely remembered Alma telling me that her wee fella wasn't all that academic, and the great advantage of Craigmillan was, it isn't really a grammar school at all, it takes all sorts . . . but mostly the wealthier sorts . . . And with them living so close to Craigmillan, it made sense for Ross to go there, instead of having to do a massive drive round every morning with his mum, taking a detour to drop him off at Unity High on her way to Unity Primary.

'Craigmillan,' I said. 'But isn't it awful far away from where you live?'

'Too right, kid,' she said.

'After Derek dropped this bombshell, d'you know I actually drove round there yesterday morning, through all the rush hour traffic, just to see how long it would take? Forty minutes. I kid you not. And it would take even longer if he had to get one bus into town, and another one out. We're not that close to a bus stop. No, I'd have to drive him, that's an eighty-minute round trip, twice a day.'

'How would that work out with your job . . . '

'Job. Ha. D'you know, I still haven't told Derek I've got a job?'

'Honestly?' I said. 'D'you reckon he'd be violently against it?'

'Nah,' she sighed. 'It's not like he wants me to be one of those Stepford Wives, you know, beautifying the home all day. It's just he'd think working in a café's so . . . I don't know . . . trivial. Demeaning.' She sat up. There she was, the impeccable Alex Masterton, chewing her fingernails just like Sandra Gilroy used to do.

'No, Derek's got a plan. He says it would actually be cheaper to board him than spend a small fortune on petrol, or God forbid, taxis. Besides, if you want to board your kid, he'll definitely get in, they want the money from those boarders, they're not fussed about what grades they got in the Transfer.' Boarding school. Denzil. Well, he'd enjoy the woodland, if the boys were let rake about in it, if they weren't kept out of it on the grounds of Health and Safety. Other than that, I just couldn't picture it. Denzil. Boarding school. Two words that just didn't seem to fit in the same sentence. God love him, I thought, he's still wet behind the ears.

'He'd hate it, Vinny. He'd only be ten years, three months when he started and he'd be completely out of his depth, oh I don't mean academically, he's used to that, but emotionally . . . he's just not ready. Oh, he's not shy, he's a very sociable wee soul, but he needs his down time, kicking a ball against the wall and telling himself wee stories when he thinks no-one's listening . . . and an all-boy environment, 24/7, it would just increase his lack of confidence, and what if he gets bullied? Right now he tells me pretty much everything. Well, everything that needs dealt with, that is. But if he goes away to boarding school and the big lads are making his life hell, how's he going to tell me that? Write me a letter? This isn't the 1950s. Or ring up and . . . ? He wouldn't, you know. Dear love him, he wouldn't want to worry me, he'd just suffer in silence . . . '

Her nail varnish was getting ruined, I said 'Does Derek not realise?'

'No,' she said sourly, 'Derek obviously thinks it would be good for Denzil to be away from me. His airhead dumb blonde mother. I believe he genuinely thinks I'm somehow holding Denzil back'

There was a long, agonising silence.

No use me saying 'Well, of course you're not holding him back' because that wasn't the point; the point was that she thought that he thought . . .

I said gently, 'I think they have weekly boarders, he could come home at weekends.'

'Weekends, well that would suit Derek. He could have a wee session with Denzil, every Saturday morning before he goes off to play his interminable golf games, quiz him about how he's getting on, what sort of marks is he getting, is he shaping up OK? And then he wouldn't have to be bothered with him for the rest of the week, while I'd be worrying my head off.'

And suddenly the thirty minutes were up. Denzil and Roisin burst out of the house, insisting we watch them do the entire assault course, starting precariously on the car port roof, and ending with them swinging down from the big apple tree to bounce on the trampoline, unable to travel any further without setting foot on the ground.

'What we need,' Denzil suggested, 'are some crates like they have in the Cubs. We could pile them up like a fortress and get across the back of the house that way.'

Alex said firmly that the patio would be for partygoers to mingle, and put their drinks down on the windowsills, and no crates were to be dumped at the back of the house until the party was over. Denzil looked frustrated and asked, when would it be over, and I said soon, only one more week and then he could make all the fortresses he liked, and he said, promise? And I said, yes, definitely. Promise.

Of course, after lunch, we went to the beach. So there wasn't any more time for me and Alex to talk about all that stuff, just time for Alex to mutter in my ear 'I won't give up on this, you know. I won't let Derek do this. I won't. I'll wear him down in the end.'

Crawfordsburn was a bit spoiled, because the glaring sun had brought out hundreds of teenagers, there was really loud music and kids staggering about, out of their heads on vodka, or something worse, but we walked round the bay and up the little hill and on to the next beach, and it was peaceful because it was obviously out of the reach of most of them. Denzil and Roisin paddled up to their knees, and then of course he fell over and got completely soaked, and after swimming wildly about in his clothes for a bit, he had to be dragged out by his mum.

Roisin was shivering but Denzil was elated, as if he was drunk too, not on vodka but on sea water, he kept going on about how much he loved the sea and how when they went to his Aunty Jo's house in Portrush, there were these massive big waves, and Alex was clucking because although we'd brought plenty of towels, Denzil didn't have any spare dry clothes, so we had to trek back to the car, running the gauntlet of the drunken teenagers, and what with all the carry-on, I completely forgot what I was going to ask Alex: what was she planning to do about her frisky new job, over the summer? Had she even thought? Was she simply going to take two months off Lunch at Louisa's? Or would she be making poor Denzil sit in the kitchen every day, with the chefs falling over him, while he did his eleven-plus papers?

And the party kept getting closer and closer. Alex had marvelled at my list, there were actually thirty five who'd said they'd come, I didn't know I knew so many, and it damn well better not rain because there was only standing room in the downstairs of my house for twenty, at the most. Alex was really helpful, she took me to the off-licence in the car and we bought a dozen bottles of wine and an infinity of crisps; I stopped her as she was hefting a crate of beer, she said didn't my friends drink beer, and I said well if they did they could bring it themselves, because I didn't want masses of beer cans left over after the party, I couldn't stand the stuff.

And then, the night before, the excuses started coming in. 'Sorry we can't make it after all, John's elderly mum is in hospital in Coleraine and we have to go up and see her. Sorry I can't come, Mrs McCann landed me with a whole pile of pupil profiles to do before Monday, I'd no idea she wanted them so early, I'm going to be head down all weekend. Sorry but I'm definitely getting the flu, I won't be able to stir out of the house. . .'

By Saturday, my bulging thirty five plus list had slimmed down to twenty five and I was hoping it didn't get any thinner, or this could turn out to be a really embarrassing night.

And then just a couple of hours before the party, I got a slightly odd text from Alex.

> Is it alright if I bring him? He insists on coming. x

Well, why hadn't she just asked me after Denzil's session that morning? Naturally I assumed Denzil would be coming. And I broke off from mopping the kitchen floor to scold Roisin for walking on the edge of it, and to remind her to try and make Denzil feel included, because she'd been to one or two grown-up parties in her young life, but he almost certainly hadn't, and it might be a bit awkward for him, and she said she and Zoe would be very busy, but she'd do her best, maybe Denzil could take round a plate of something, and wasn't it a bit late to be washing the kitchen floor, shouldn't that have been done earlier?

She sounded such a wee old woman, such a wee old teacher woman, all I could do was laugh and hug her, and say of course it should, it should have been done weeks ago, and nobody was going to look at the floor anyway, were they? And after that, I felt so much calmer, I didn't even get in a bate when Roisin's apron of her waitress costume came unstitched and at the last minute, she wanted me to sew it on again. Of course, the last minute is usually a long, long one; I hadn't actually given a party since before Roisin was born, but I remembered how long the wait can be, when the time you put on the invitations has come and gone, and still nobody's appeared and you wonder is anybody coming at all?

But then like a miracle, the doorbell rang, actually five minutes early. Only it wasn't a wee miracle, as it turned out, it was the veg man and Renata. So it must be true, then, about Germans and punctuality? Because it certainly wouldn't have been his idea to turn up at five to seven; must have been hers. Roisin came in with Zoe, in their cute little cartoon waitress outfits, she introduced the veg man importantly as 'This is Chris. He's Not a Teacher', and pressed a plate of canapés on him and Renata, and watched avidly while they ate them. She ignored Renata and asked Chris a series of questions about birds.

And where was Alex? She was meant to be there at the very start; it was now ten past seven, and still no sign of her. I was too embarrassed to meet anybody's eye, I just kept my head down chopping carrots and celery for the dip, drinking wine too fast, having this weird kind of internal imaginary conversation with Alex, saying *I was gobsmacked, I wouldn't have thought Chris had a partner, her saying Why not, me saying Well he has this kind of little boy lost look, like he needs looking after, her saying, Oh that sounds familiar, didn't you used to say something like that about Rory; I was obviously wrong about you and Chris, it would never have worked out, the last thing you need is another man child to look after, me saying Oh for goodness sake, Alex, I'm not an idiot, I'm perfectly capable of running my own affairs, or not affairs actually in this case,* and gulping down more wine . . .

Then Paul, our VP, turned up with his wife, whom I'd never met; I thought is this going to turn into one of those Bridget-Jones-dinner-party things, with everybody in couples? Paul addressed Roisin and Zoe in a rather falsely jolly, patronising sort of way, causing Zoe to convulse with giggles and Roisin to drag her out into the garden and start scolding her. Soon there were more teachers, all happily knocking back the cheap Shiraz and discussing their summer holiday plans, and I realised my party wasn't going to be a total disaster, but I also realised I would be on my feet for the next four hours and I might as well be teaching wriggly little P3s who can't sit still and you have to keep walking round them all the time.

Roisin came in, complaining 'There's far too many teachers, it's a bit embarrassing for Zoe,' and I said, 'Oh for goodness sake, go and talk to that woman who came with Chris, she's probably the only one who isn't a teacher.'

Roisin marched up to her, asking in her most sophisticated manner 'What do you do?' and Renata replied in her dry, precise voice, loud enough to carry across the room, 'I grow vegetables. And I sell them. But not for much longer.'

She began to talk animatedly about her new job, in Dusseldorf, which still seemed to involve vegetables but this time they were frozen, and it was all to do with PR and marketing, I couldn't quite make out the details as I wove in and out of various conversations, but it all sounded very international. I noticed she wasn't wearing the dungarees any more. She looked smarter, more glossy and businesslike, as if she were already dressed for travelling, or PR and marketing, whatever that involved, and I tried to picture Chris dressed up semi-smartly for that kind of job, and failed utterly.

A fridge magnet fell onto the floor and sort of bounced, you wouldn't think a fridge magnet could do that, it ended up right under the radiator and Roisin and Zoe both scrabbled for it. I realised that Chris was pulling off the fridge magnets one by one and examining them, as if he'd never seen them before, and sticking them back again. Renata was staring at him. *She wants him to look at her*, I thought. But he wouldn't. She refilled her glass and headed out into the garden. Chris put down his glass on the worktop, picked it up again, looked helplessly round for some more wine, couldn't see any, put the glass down again and eventually followed her. Through the window I could see them arguing, Renata striding about the lawn and Chris standing completely still, he kept shrugging his shoulders and kind of turning his palms up and outwards in a 'What-do-you-expect-me-to-do' sort of gesture, but luckily the window was closed, so none of their words carried back to where I was standing.

Then suddenly Alex was there, in a jangle of bracelets and a big gust of perfume; I was sure it wasn't Life is Beautiful this time, it was something much more assertive and predatory, Poison or Addict or Opium or . . . ? Behind her was Denzil, looking uncharacteristically embarrassed, then Derek. Why on earth had she brought Derek? Was this who she'd meant, when she'd said 'He insists on coming?' And why would he insist? Apart from occasions that might get into the *Ulster Tatler*, he hardly ever seemed to get round to actually going out with her. Why was he making an exception in my case?

At first it was alright. He graciously accepted a glass of the cheap Shiraz, as if it was something much more expensive. He started heading out into the garden, but seeing only Chris and Renata, still apparently arguing, he turned round on the doorstep and headed back in. Or maybe it was the sight of the dead rowan tree with bits of rope hanging out of it, the ancient apple tree behind it smothered in Russian vines, and all those brambles bursting out on to the shaggy lawn. And I was standing behind him, apologising to his back: 'Oh I'm afraid it's all a terrible mess and a muddle, but what the heck . . . I like to think all that rampant unchecked growth is sort of creative . . . '

He gave me a politely surprised look and turned back into the kitchen, examining Roisin's drawings on the fridge. There was another new one, that I hadn't seen before – had she been creeping down before breakfast to stick up her drawings? It looked like an inverted top hat, with green leafy stems growing out of it, wrapping themselves round table legs and chairs and sort of dripping from the ceiling, bursting out into great pink blossoms, so that they looked like an implausible cross between vines and rhododendrons.

'And what is that, young lady?' Derek asked.

'I know!' Denzil burst out. 'It's the hobgoblin's hat!'

'It's from the Finn Family Moomintroll book,' Roisin explained graciously, emphasising the word 'book' slightly, to pre-empt any suggestion that she might have been watching DVDs aimed at four year olds.

'What happens is, it's a magic hat and it changes things, Moominmamma puts bits of flowers into it and they turn into vines and creepers and grow all over the house and there's masses of flowers and fruit everywhere and there's so much stuff growing, you can hardly even see the house . . . '

'I know!' Denzil said again, delighted. 'I read that too! But then didn't it all disappear? When the sun went down, didn't the plants all shrivel up, and the Moomins burnt them all in a big fire?'

'Well, no doubt it was a relief to get back to normal,' said Derek. 'And it isn't strictly true to say that you read it, surely? Didn't your mother read it to you?'

Denzil actually went quite red, and I thought, what's wrong with the man? Doesn't he have any rapport with the kid at all?

Roisin and Zoe disappeared into the garden, where a few more people were now beginning to gather, and started handing round crisps. Denzil looked longingly after them.

'Ah, go on out,' said Alex, 'but *no* climbing on all that stuff while the grown-ups are out there, OK?'

She handed him a big plate of smiley face crackers. 'Now, pass these round and don't come back in till they're all eaten!'

She took Derek's arm, without making eye contact, and steered him towards a little knot of teachers in the sitting room. I couldn't imagine what he could find in common with any of them, but there seemed to be quite a lively conversation developing. She left him to it, and came back and hugged me.

'Sorry I had to bring him,' she said. 'I'll explain later. Do you want those in the oven?'

'What? Oh, the bacon pinwheels . . . sure. . . there's a baking tray in the cupboard.'

She set to enthusiastically. It was just as well Chris

was out in the garden; she didn't have the sight of him to annoy her, and make her go all haughty. She was so relaxed, she was actually singing to herself; I could just hear her, above the buzz of conversation. Yes, buzz. Things were starting to warm up at last, and I put down my drink firmly and made myself go and talk to Josie and Martin, the couple from next door whom I'd never thought would actually come; turned out they'd been to Canada, and they claimed to have enjoyed Lake Huron every bit as much as the Rocky Mountains, which I found hard to believe, but they said they just weren't mountain types.

Only Denzil didn't seem to have found a niche for himself. Roisin and Zoe were weaving in and out of the guests, beaming, collecting compliments on what great girls they were, so helpful, but Denzil was just hanging about on the edge of things, like the saying goes: hanging about with one arm longer than the other. In fact, one arm actually was longer, because the other was awkwardly holding the plate of smiley face crackers. As I watched, he stumped over to the stone terrace and sat there, gazing at the chattering guests, still cradling the plate. I couldn't see his face, but in the way he was sitting I could see dejection and gloom and the early stirrings of pre-teenage alienation. Then he started picking the wee shrimps off the crackers. I averted my eyes.

I couldn't see Chris at all, but Renata had come back in, and was in the little knot of people Derek was talking to, round the fireplace. I was stuck with Josie and Martin, who'd finished with Lake Huron now and were talking about their holiday home in Portrush, not nearly so interesting. I could hear scraps of conversation drifting over from the group round the fireplace; it seemed to be all about education, with Renata's voice carrying just as much as any of the men's: 'holistic – the whole child—' I heard her say, and then 'Art. Creativity. Things that are important.'

For a moment, I envied the way she could dominate a room – I wished I could – though I can, too, I suppose. But only a classroom. Not any other kind of room. And then I heard Derek say 'So if integrated schools are all-ability, that surely means the slower children are holding back the brighter ones? Does it not affect their A-level results?' Paul's voice started up in response; I knew he had a son at Unity High, who was doing very well, I thought Go on ya boy ye, just you tell him!

After a few more minutes of this, Derek came over to the kitchen end of the room to refill his glass. He wouldn't think to look out into the garden to see how Denzil was getting on, would he? Maybe go and chat to him for a bit? Of course not. I glanced out of the window. Oh, Lord. Denzil was still sitting in the same position, but the plate was now empty. He obviously hadn't been handing the crackers round. He must have eaten the lot. Was this what his life was going to be like for the next ten years – baffled, out of it, not quite up to things? Always hovering disconsolately at the edge of the real action, the place where the smart people were holding court, the bright ones, the winners? Getting passed over, and getting fatter and fatter?

Derek was hovering over me, wanting to confirm that his wife had told me Denzil would have to come next Monday afternoon instead of Tuesday, because of the parent teacher afternoon at his school, and when I said oh, she must have forgotten to mention it, he gave an exasperated sigh, like a parent huffing over a recalcitrant child. He offered, with stiff politeness, to refill my glass; it must have been my third or fourth refill.

I took a big gulp and found myself saying to him 'You know, I've been wondering for a while now. Did you ask Alex to have that nose job? What did you say to her, exactly?'

He drew himself up. Normally he had a bit of a stoop, but he was actually a good six inches taller than me.

'Mrs Corcoran, I can't believe what I just heard you say. In the first place, it is plainly none of your business, and in the second place, do you have any idea how much these operations cost? We had one child in P1 at prep school and another starting soon. It was a considerable financial sacrifice. Wouldn't have been my choice.'

He looked scathingly across at Alex, who was chatting about cafés in Portrush with Josie and Martin, talking animatedly and jangling her bangles. And although she wasn't aware of him, I could see all her bright jangliness crumble to ash on the floor under his gaze.

'Excuse me,' I said.

There was a smell of burning. I squatted down to get the pinwheels out of the oven and a blast of hot air hit me in the face, bringing tears to my eyes. When I straightened up, Derek was gone. I stood there stupidly holding a tray of little charred, collapsed things, wondering what on earth to do with them. There was something about Derek that took twenty years off me, and not in a good way. He made me feel like a stroppy teenager – I just wanted to jump up and take a swipe at him. And there he was, back at the fireplace, chatting away to the same group again, Paul and the other guys, he seemed perfectly relaxed, I could even hear him laughing.

I stared gloomily out of the window and there was Chris, walking across the lawn. He was carrying a red plastic box, which I recognised; why had he been rummaging about in those heaps of old junk in the car port? He said something to Denzil, who got up and followed him to the other side of the garden. Chris put the box down under the old rhododendron, then walked back across the lawn, and he and Denzil took out the contents: a dozen brightly coloured plastic balls.

They were for a game of boules like the French play, you were supposed to roll one and then roll another one after it, so that the second ball would gently nudge the first ball out of the way. But our lawn was too bumpy, the balls wouldn't roll, they bucked wildly and bounced in all directions.

Chris obviously had a better idea. He stood on the patio with his back to the house, and carefully bowled one of the balls so that it almost – almost – made it into the box. Only it bumped a low hanging rhododendron branch, and flumped down into the tangled undergrowth. I could hear Chris say 'Darn', pretending disgust at his own hopelessness. Denzil's turn appeared to go better; he actually got his ball into the box; Chris reacted with exaggerated delight, and the two of them high-fived each other. I laughed. It was so simple, but brilliant. Two schoolboys, a real one and a pretend one, happily ignoring the boring adult conversation with all its undercurrents and incomprehensibilities. I was still laughing when Alex came over to me. I'd been wrong: she wasn't crumbling to ash. She was beaming.

'Vinny! He's agreed! He's agreed! He says Denzil can go to the integrated school! To Unity High!'

I could hear all the exclamation marks in her

speech, just like I could sometimes hear all the commas in Derek's. I stared at her, gobsmacked, my mouth hanging open.

She just rattled on, 'It's why I had to bring him, because I kept trying to talk him into it and he was really sniffy about it, and I said there'd be people at your party who have kids at Unity High, and there actually are, three of them, and the kids are all doing really well and one of them just got six As and two Bs in her GCSEs, and Derek's convinced, isn't it great!'

He came up behind her. He said stiffly, without meeting my eye, 'Under the circumstances, it is beginning to look like the best solution.'

I couldn't let this go on.

I took a deep breath and said 'They're oversubscribed. They always are. Last year they had two hundred and sixty eight applications for two hundred places.'

Alex froze. Derek put down his glass.

I went on, 'So they have to give priority to kids who've been to an integrated primary school. And after that, kids who've already got brothers or sisters at Unity, or only children of course, but if they've already got brothers or sisters at another school, it means . . . ' my voice trailed off.

'Yes, I can see exactly what it means' Derek said in a flat, tired voice. So what you're trying to tell us is, Denzil wouldn't get in.'

'No. He wouldn't. He doesn't meet a single one of the criteria, I'm so sorry—'

There was silence.

Then Derek said 'This is June, Mrs Corcoran. You've been talking to my wife about integrated education for three months now, and you never once thought to tell her that Denzil couldn't even get into the damn integrated school?'

'I haven't – we haven't—'

I heard myself flustering as if I had something to feel guilty about.

He'd gone very white under his skiing-and-golfing tan.

He stared at Alex with an infinite, weary disdain.

'What the hell are we supposed to do? I should have stood over him, the way I did with the other two. Instead, I left you to sort it all out, and look where that's got us, he's going to end up just like you.'

She flushed. 'What's that supposed to mean?'

'Well, unless he goes to boarding school, what's he going to do? Go to Rushfield and then go to the Tech and do a plumbing course or something? I mean, he can hardly do what you did, can he? In spite of all the liberated claptrap there is nowadays, I hardly think the option of catching a rich husband will be open to him.'

For a moment, I thought she was going to slap his face. But she gulped, turned away from him and stared out the window. There was an astonishing pink sunset, with a glory of gold and apricot starting slowly to fade; Paul had marshalled everybody out into the garden to admire it, but I don't think she even saw it.

Derek said bitterly, 'That's right, just stand there staring out the window as if it's got nothing to do with you. That's your answer to everything, isn't it? Stare out the bloody window. I suppose you were staring out the bloody window when you were meant to be doing the eleven-plus.'

I couldn't stand any more of this; I bolted upstairs, pressed my face against the window in the front bedroom, feeling the glass cool against my forehead. But then it was too cold, I was shivering, actually shivering. His mean little eyes, I could still see them, glaring at her. His exhausted eyes. Barren and bleak as a winter's day . . .

The windows are high in our school hall, too high to see out of. They have criss-cross wires on them, in case anybody throws stones outside, or there's a bomb. We sit at separate desks, with acres of empty space all round us, and it feels strange. We're used to being crammed into a small classroom, all thirty five of us, grouped round tables, sharing pencils and rubbers, chattering all the time. Arguing. Laughing. Now there's a strained silence, as we wait for the invigilator to tell us to turn our papers over. I know Sandra's right behind me. I don't look round. Before the first test, she said she had to go to the toilets because she felt sick. I didn't feel sick. I was very proud of that. Now I don't want to look at Sandra, in case she looks like she's feeling sick, and in case that makes me feel sick too.

So I look towards the high windows again, gazing at the grey November sky, soft grey criss-crossed with lines. Then I see something amazing. Dirty white flakes meandering down across the greyness, at first just one or two, then more and more. The invigilator's voice snaps 'Turn your papers over and start! You have one hour!' I know I have to be half way through by ten o'clock. I've practised this so often at home, with my Mum looking strained and anxious, my Dad saying 'Never mind, you'll do fine. Just make sure you finish in time. Just whatever you do, don't get distracted. Con-cen-trate.' So I concentrate, and when I pause at ten o'clock to take ten slow, deep breaths, like my Dad said, that's the first time I look round. There's Sandra, her wee face turned up towards the window, apparently mesmerised by the random flakes which are still sifting very slowly down across the glass. I will it to stop snowing, or I will her to stop looking at it, but I know I can't do anything about it, I remember what my Dad said, after the ten deep breaths I just have to get my nose pointing right down to the page again. Then I hear the invigilator say, 'Never mind the snow, P7. You'll have all day to look at it afterwards. No more looking out the windows now. Look down. Everybody. Look down.' So that's alright, she'll be looking down, she'll be OK.

When we get finished, I grab my pencil case and my cardigan and I'm the first out the door, I want to see the snow, and there's still a few desultory flakes drifting down, and I try and catch them on my tongue. Then Sandra comes up to me. Her face is all wet and I realise it isn't the snow. It's tears. She says 'I didn't get finished. I couldn't stop looking out the window. It was the snow. It put me off.' She blows her nose with a dirty Kleenex. 'I'm going home.' One of the teachers shouts after her, because you're not supposed to go home unless your mum or dad or granny comes for you. But she's already out the gate and away. I stand there on my own, my cheeks cooling and my hands getting frozen without gloves, and by this time the snow has stopped, there's only a dirty white frosting left on the tarmac and it soon turns to slush, and that day there's no more snow and the day after and the day after and so on for weeks and then for the rest of the winter, as if the snow felt guilty for spoiling everything, as if it didn't want to come back.

A noise woke me up from that cold, shivery place of thirty years ago. It was a door banging: my front door. I could see Alex striding down the path, with her very fast I-should-have-been-a-PE-teacher stride, Denzil trotting behind her. She turned round and grabbed his hand. He resisted, as any normal ten year old boy would naturally resist if his Mum wanted to hold his hand in public. But she kept hold of the hand firmly, and positively dragged him along. She must be parked quite far from the house, she'd arrived so late. Because the bedroom window doesn't open out very far, once she'd gone past the first few neighbours' houses I could no longer see her, but soon I heard a car revving up. So she'd taken whichever of their glossy pair of cars she and Derek had arrived in, and driven off. Which left Derek to do what – get a taxi?

I really didn't want to meet his accusing eyes. Scathing. At least, if eyes could be scathing – well, his probably could. But it was my party; I had to reappear at it. halfway down the stairs I met Roisin coming up, looking indignant.

'Denzil's gone home!' she said.

'Well, it must be getting on for ten o'clock.'

'But we were going to do the Wilderness Course!'

'Well, you and Zoe can go out there and do it, now the people are coming back in.'

She glowered. 'Zoe isn't really into things like that. Me and Denzil were going to do it. To show her. And to show the veg man, but he said he had to go.'

I made a what-am-I-supposed-to-do-about-it gesture, went across to the sink and ran the cold tap. I would spend the rest of the evening drinking tap water in a wine glass. Soon I'd be sober, well near enough, there'd be no more embarrassing outbursts, well not on my part anyway. I'd look quite presentable when Zoe's Mum arrived to take her away, and I'd be able to face Derek with a clear head, and say . . . what on earth was I going to say?

But there was no sign of him. The guests trooped in from the garden, they milled about, drank more wine, I made coffee. Alma McCrory, rolling up her flowery summer sleeves, nobly started washing up, and I said Of course you mustn't, and she said Of course I must. People were starting to leave, and still no sign of Derek.

Had he ordered a taxi? I hadn't heard one arrive. Had he simply walked off, heading down our street, on to the main road, looking for a bus stop, a taxi rank, a pub? The thought of Derek, in his expensive linen summer jacket and glossy shirt and those pale beige shoes that looked as new as if he'd never worn them before, walking down our homely wee street, was somehow almost more disturbing than anything else that had happened.

During the night, when I was trying to get to sleep and everything was churning round in my head, I remembered the woman I'd seen him in the Pirate's Head. Maybe she didn't live in a grand house up the Malone Road; maybe she lived somewhere in our wee suburb, and he'd gone over there to tell her all about it? Well, that wouldn't do him much good, unless she was some kind of educational expert. I couldn't see anywhere Denzil could go, except Rushfield or boarding school, and Alex was right. He'd hate it.

I lay awake and worried, drifting in and out of sleep, having endless arguments in my head with Alex, with Derek, even with Denzil, trying to convince him he'd enjoy boarding at Campbell, well maybe not at first, but in the long run it would be better . . . in the long run . . . not even in my half-dreaming state could I get Denzil to visualise the long run, and when I tried to look ahead myself, I didn't like it much either.

Then I woke up and it was light. A glorious early summer morning. Suddenly, I was in the garden and everything was so bright, each leaf looked like a child had drawn it and coloured it in, incredibly carefully, with the most garish crayons he could find. But I thought, where are the birds? It's summer, it's dawn, shouldn't there be a dawn chorus? It was utterly silent. I slunk back into the house and there were the birds, my kitchen was full of them, but they weren't singing, just crawling about, as if they'd forgotten how to fly. I opened the window to see if they'd go out, but they didn't seem to like it, just started making an angry sort of buzzing noise.

Then I turned round and after all, there was only one bird, but it was huge, it practically came up to my waist, it was slim and dark with long wings and a tail trailing sadly on the ground, I thought Oh no it's a swift, they're meant to spend all their lives in the air and if it gets stuck on the ground it will die, but then it smiled and I no longer questioned how a bird could smile, I just thought Oh that's alright, it's a swallow, but there was something about its smile I didn't like, I sort of backed away from it, and then I was going up the stairs but it somehow got past me into the bedroom, it turned round and smiled at me again and it very slowly and deliberately opened the wardrobe door, and inside there was a sort of road works going on, there were men in yellow hard hats and flashing lights and machines roaring and there was a sort of thumping, the creature just went into the wardrobe and closed the door and I could still hear it, nagging away in my brain, a sort of roaring and a rustling almost as loud as the roaring and underneath it all that maddening, endless thumping.

Then I woke up, this time for real. It was light, but a way-past-dawn light, and when I got up and opened the window, there wasn't any silence; I could hear blackbirds singing, and sparrows chirping, and what sounded like a magpie scolding. I went and opened the wardrobe door, and of course it just looked like the inside of any old wardrobe, with shoes jumbled in the bottom of it and cardigans with their fuzzy long sleeves and dresses with belts trailing down.

And then Roisin appeared. The dote. Bringing me a cup of coffee in bed. Surely the first time in her life she'd ever made coffee, and she mustn't have used completely boiling water because it was tepid and had a few granules floating in it, but all the same, I was touched.

'Dad just texted to say we're all going to Newcastle, and he's picking me up early!'

'Breakfast—' I said firmly, and so I was still in my dressing gown standing over Roisin while she ate her cereal, when Rory came in, cheerily whistling. He did a double take at the sight of the dressing gown, and said, was that the same one I always used to wear . . . when . . . you know . . .

'When we were still married?' I asked. 'Yes. It's probably still the same one. Roisin gets all the new stuff.'

And then I said 'You know, Rory, we maybe should talk about money some time' and he looked embarrassed and said 'Yeah, you know what, you're right, we should, yeah, we really should talk about money some time, yeah, definitely . . . '
When they'd gone, I texted Alex.

> Hey I actually asked Rory about the child support. At least I almost asked him & he knew I was almost asking him so that's start isn't it?

No answer. After half an hour I texted again, more carefully this time.

> Sorry. That was crass, I should have asked how you are? Thinking about you. Vx

I was over-reacting. She was probably still asleep. Or she'd taken Denzil off in the car to some wee friend's house, or wherever they usually went on Sunday mornings. I made myself a fry, and then I started rinsing out beer cans and squashing them and putting them in a bag, and rinsing the bottles and putting them in another bag. I'd only bought a dozen bottles, but there were now about twenty empty ones, it must have been more of a party than I'd realised. How was I going to get this lot to the bottle bank?

I automatically started texting Alex, to see if she could take them in her car. Then I groaned, and deleted the text. Whatever state of mind Alex was in, she surely didn't want me bending her ear about empty wine bottles.

I got on with a pile of marking: there's always a pile of marking to get on with. But the house was so quiet, Sunday afternoon so long and deadly and silent, I couldn't stop myself texting again.

Is everything OK?

Well, that was stupid. Of course everything wasn't OK. But I'd sent it now. What else could I say? The silence was unnerving me. Was she alright? Well, I thought, he's hardly going to beat her up, is he? She's a tough girl, she could knock him across the room. No, it's more the emotional abuse I'd be worried about. Was she mad because I hadn't told her that Denzil wouldn't get into Unity, no, that didn't make sense, she'd never even asked me . . . was Denzil upset? Though of course he couldn't have heard Derek berating her . . . but kids can sense an atmosphere.

I took a rug and a couple of cushions and the paper; I made myself comfy on the lawn. I tried to blot all the Mastertons out of my mind. It was hot, the garden was starting to look a bit dried-out, but it also had a kind of post-party glamour: there were a couple of empty glasses on the terrace, and on the lawn a squashed cigarette butt.

Who was that? I didn't see anybody smoking. Well, anyway, some people had enjoyed themselves, it wasn't all trauma and despair. There was a blue plastic ball lodged in amongst the straggly sweet amber, right beside my head. I picked it up and aimed it into the box, which was still there. It fell short. It's hard to throw straight when you're lying propped up on one elbow.

I imagined I could see worn tracks in the grass, where Renata had been striding about. Like the tracks cats make, when they're avoiding contact with each other, stalking along paths of their own. For a moment I wondered, was she only saying all that stuff for effect? To make him . . . to make him what, exactly? Go down on one knee and propose marriage? Nah. That would hardly help. Would it? No, I thought. I had the feeling that with Renata, what you see is what you get. She's pretty direct. He's the more oblique one, more layered, I guess.

Layers. How many layers would Derek have? Frighteningly many. Though of course, he would never stride about the grass, arguing. He would just stand there in the doorway – not just my doorway, but the doorway of anyone's house, or indeed anyone's life. He would sweep the garden, or the life, with a glance. A scathing, withering glance. And then he'd turn back indoors.

I tried again, to empty my mind. To chase out all the humans, and focus only on the humming of the bees, nosing in and out of foxgloves and big floppy rhododendron blossoms. The monotonous, inanely contented chirp of the sparrows. The warmth of the sun, stroking my hair, burning my legs, I put my cardigan over them, and a bit of scruffy rug over my forehead to keep the dazzle out of my eyes.

I must have slept. I woke up with a dry mouth, a headache and my right hip all stiff from lying on the hard ground. I was standing by the kitchen sink, gulping cold water and rubbing my eyes, when Roisin came back.

'Are you very tired?' she asked, carefully.

'Yes very tired, honey, but look at all the marking I've done. And just think, only two more weeks of term left.'

'Yay!' she crowed. 'It's the show, then my party, then the Guide camp, then Canada . . . '

All evening, she prattled happily about her plans, while I made dinner and finished my marking and got ready, in grim silence, for Monday morning. Still no word from Alex, though I'd texted her twice more. Surely the least she could do was reply?

And I told myself, Don't think about it anymore, there's been way too much thinking about Alex; and I immersed myself in school and all that tired-but-happy end of term busyness, the light-at-the-end-of-the-tunnel, this-is-the-final-batch-of-maths-tests feeling, and it was fine, Monday morning, all the reassuring old grumbles, the kids writing their last story of the term, the rain finally starting and nosing down the window panes, and it felt all closed down and peaceful, it was like battening down the hatches, like zipping shut the door of a great big sleepy tent.

Until I got off the bus, and I got that text, and Roisin met me, and everything was suddenly blown wide open.

MONDAY 15 JUNE

She hears a vehicle draw up outside. She is still clutching the cushion, and she puts it down carefully, stands up, waiting for the doorbell to ring. Nothing. But she can see a head and shoulders through the frosted glass: a tall figure. Her stomach lurches as she thinks maybe it's Derek. She backs away, towards the fireplace, and then sees the van: Locally Organic. She feels all the tension drain out of her.

She opens the door to Chris, who's still struggling to find the doorbell: usually, when he arrives, the door is already ajar. He is empty-handed.

'No vegetables?'

'That's tomorrow,' he says. 'I only came because she phoned me.'

'Who? Alex?'

'Yeah, the thing is . . . ' he sits heavily down on the sofa. 'I went round there this morning with a box of veg. Since she started that job, I just key in the number and the gates open themselves and I go in and leave the box at the back door. Only, there was a hell of a noise, the burglar alarm going off, I walked round to the conservatory and it was all broken glass. Half a dozen windows had been smashed and I thought, why would a burglar bother breaking more than one? There was glass all over the floor inside, but it didn't look like anything had been taken. And I stood there thinking, what do I do here, should I phone her, should I phone the police? And then, it was very weird, she phoned me. Didn't even know she had my mobile number.'

'What did she say?'

'I couldn't really make it out – the signal kept cutting out. Sounded like she was on the edge of nowhere. She just kept saying, tell Vinny to go on Skype, that's the only bit I could make out because she kept repeating it, like she was walking about trying different places to get a signal, and then there were all these crashing noises—' he sees Vinny's worried look – 'no, not like breaking glass. Sounded more like waves.'

Vinny lets out a long sigh. Waves. Where the hell is Alex? On a beach somewhere, while she, Vinny, is facing a dead expanse of mud? Chris says he'll go out and look at it. See if there's anything there that can be salvaged. And Vinny trundles upstairs, to throw Roisin off the computer, she should have done this in the first place, she has to skype

Alex right now, find out what the hell's been going on. But there, on the landing, she stops dead. It's Denzil's voice, loud and clear, he sounds as if he's in the very room with Roisin – 'And I'm going to surf school—' For a mad moment she thinks maybe he's really there, that Alex somehow got him into the house while she, Vinny, was gurning into a cushion –

She edges up to the doorway, keeping well to one side, so the computer won't catch her on wherever it keeps its sneaky little camera. She peers in.

On the screen is Denzil's face, flushed and beaming; behind him a pale beige background, with a line of blue across the top, broken up by little scraps of white. It looks like he's on a beach, but they don't have WiFi on beaches, surely? It must be through a window, he's sitting with his back to a window, where the hell is he?

And Roisin says, 'How can you do surfing at school? Wouldn't the swimming pool be too small?'

Denzil grins.

'No, it's an outdoors school. If there's not enough waves you do games on the beach and beach safety and then you have a packed lunch and then if there's enough waves you can do surfing in the afternoon and I'm doing it in July because my mum's going to get a job in a café and for the last bit of June I'm going to help my Mum look after my aunty Joanne's dog and her twins and they're going away in August but it's only for two weeks and we'll still be looking after the dog.'

This is the longest speech Vinny's ever heard Denzil make. She backs off to the landing. Stands at the top of the stairs. Baffled. Is Alex with him? She must be, because Denzil surely couldn't have got to this place, this beach wherever it is, on his own? She thinks, *I'll let them rattle on for a bit, before I go and interrupt them. Alex can wait, for a few minutes anyway. She doesn't seem to be in a very hasty sort of place. Not now.*

Vinny hears Roisin answering, then Denzil again, then Roisin laughing. She tiptoes down the stairs. Chris, oddly, is sitting at the kitchen table with a sheet of paper in front of him. As she comes in, he half turns and casually puts his arm across it, so she can't see what he's been doing; like the kids at school when they're drawing something instead of doing sums. She sits down on the sofa, but this time stays upright; no curling up, and definitely no tears.

She says, 'What on earth is Alex up to? She appears to be taking Denzil out of school for the last couple of weeks. How's that going to help anyone? Is she cracking up altogether?'

'To be honest, no, I wouldn't think so,' Chris says. 'What little I know of her, she isn't as dumb or as blonde as she likes to appear. She quite possibly has a plan. In spite of all that broken glass. Or maybe the broken glass is even part of the plan.'

Vinny shakes her head, in bewilderment. She looks at Chris, and the sheet of paper he's half-heartedly trying to conceal. 'What's that, then?' Chris grins sheepishly.

'Also a plan. Sort of. I mean, there's nothing salvageable out there, it's just basically a ploughed field, and I was just kind of . . . sketching something out . . . not that it's any of my business, obviously.'

Vinny looks at him disbelievingly. She goes over to the window and stares out. The rain has stopped, and in the middle of the mangled expanse of mud, a pigeon has alighted. It stalks importantly about, head bobbing backwards and forwards. It pauses, half turns, regards her with a beady eye. Then it continues strutting; the head goes down and it stabs at something; the beak points up skywards, the head makes a tossing motion; the beak stabs down again into the mass of roots and mud. And so it goes on. It can't be finding anything to eat in all that mess, surely?

Vinny turns back to Chris. 'It's honestly pretty hopeless—'

Roisin bursts in. She is fizzing with excitement, words tumbling out nineteen to the dozen, bouncing from one subject to another and back again, she's caught the bug from Denzil and is even less coherent than he is. surf school, his aunty's dog, holiday homes, the dog again, his aunty's twins, caravans, Cub camp, wetsuits . . .

'And he says we can hire wetsuits. And he says we can go and stay! After Canada! Can we? Can we?'

'Stay where?'

'In his aunty's house. When they're away. I told you.'

She catches sight of Chris and says, rather rudely, 'What are you doing here?'

'Helping,' he replies gravely.

'Oh. Is Renata here, she said she'd give me her Staedtler paint box if she went back to Germany, is she going back?'

'Yes. She's gone to say goodbye to my mother.'

'That's nice,' says Roisin, more politely.

'Extremely.'

Suddenly Roisin reverts to her usual organising self. 'Oh, I meant to say right away. His Mum wants to talk to you. Denzil's Mum. She's on Skype. Can you go up now?'

'Of course,' says Vinny.

She leaves them to it and bounds back upstairs, and there is Alex, framed against a background of sand and waves, the same way Denzil had been earlier. In the last few minutes, the sun seems to have got stronger; it's blinding. At the sight of all that sand, smooth and unploughed up, Vinny feels resentment and anger surfacing again. But Alex looks hag-ridden and exhausted. She doesn't seem to be wearing any make-up, and her eyes are a bit red as if she's been rubbing them, maybe she just got sand in them or maybe she's been crying?

And the first thing she says is, 'Oh, Vinny, I'm so sorry, I just couldn't believe it.'

'What?'

'He texted me, he actually texted me a photo – I'd kept the phone switched off ever since I left, and the minute I switched it on again, there was this photo of a digger in your back garden and a big pile of rubble that used to be your terrace, and all your lovely trees and wild bushes, and just all mud and stuff where they used to be—'

'Are you saying Derek's been round at my place?'

'Yes, he sometimes finishes work early on Mondays and usually he . . . sees private patients, or so he says, but this time he . . . '

Yuk, she thinks. He must have missed Roisin by a whisker. Because Roisin would surely have said, if she'd encountered Derek taking photos on his phone, such a weird thing to do.

'Why?' Vinny asks.

And Alex says, 'It was the only way he could get at me. I trashed his place, so he was going to trash mine. Just like two maladjusted kids, isn't it? Only I didn't have a place of my own. Everything I had was his. So he came to your place, I used to talk about how happy I was in your wild garden and how I could relax there better than anywhere else, and he never listens to me much, but some of it must have gone in.'

'What do you mean, you trashed his place?'

She blows her nose. Makes visible efforts to pull herself together.

'Oh, Vinny, you should have heard the stuff he was coming out with. We'd both had a sleepless night, pretty much, and in the morning he just kept going on and on at me – he said if Denzil didn't go to boarding school, he'd end up somewhere like Rushfield with all the layabouts, and his life would never amount to anything – and I said, Well I went to Rushfield, remember? And I seem to have survived – and then he said – you wouldn't believe—'

'What?'

'He said, You! Dear God I'd shoot him, if I thought he wasn't going to achieve more than you have! You're forty two and all you've ever done is nursing and you only stuck at that for four years, I seem to remember.'

Vinny shivers. 'Are you sure he said that?'

Alex stares at her soberly.

'Quite sure. Because you know the awful thing? He wasn't even shouting. He was kind of saying it all through clenched teeth, in a horrible sort of quiet, deliberate voice. He looked like a man who'd just shot some kind of wee furry animal, and now he's skinning it and cutting it up, piece by piece. That's what he was doing – quietly, deliberately sawing our marriage to bits. And the more he was quiet, the more I was screaming at him – I said, I raised your children didn't I?

'And he said, "Well even the Traveller women up the Glen Road can do that!" And I said, "Jesus, don't you have any respect for me at all?" – And he said, "Get a grip, Alexandra, we're not talking about you, we're talking about Denzil," and I said, "Did you ever have any respect for me, did you always see me as some kind of glamorised unpaid skivvy with half a brain," and he said it again, "Don't be so pathetically self-absorbed, we need to talk about Denzil, this isn't the time to be talking about you," and I just said, "Well when is it going to be time, Derek? When?"

'Then I grabbed this great big Waterford crystal vase he'd given me for my birthday once, which to be honest I'd always pretty much hated, and I smashed it on the floor.'

There are tears in her eyes again, and Vinny wants to reach out and hug her, this frantic angry child woman, but you can't hug a screen. Alex draws a deep breath, and continues,

'And you know that song from the nineteen eighties – "I love the sound of breaking glass, I hear it in my dreams" – well it was like that, it was . . .

just the most delicious sound ever. And then Denzil came in, he was still in his pyjamas, he'd heard the noise and he looked . . . Well, he looked scared. And you know what?'

'What?'

'It might have changed things, even at that stage, if Derek had said . . . if he'd showed any kind of emotion . . . but he wouldn't even look at me. Or Denzil. He just looked at the broken glass, and then he said, I have to go to work in five minutes. I expect to find that all cleared up when I get back. Then he just walked off, and I told Denzil to get dressed and pack some stuff, we were going to the North Coast, and he just slunk off still looking scared, poor wee soul.'

Vinny is still trying to make sense of it all.

'So,' she says slowly, 'when you said that you trashed his place . . . '

'I broke all the windows in the Sun Room.' She stares at Vinny defiantly. 'With those marble eggs, you know those wee things that're on a table out there in a big glass bowl, they're really heavy, they'd break anything – Oh, Vinny, I had to do it.'

'Why?'

'Because . . . well, winters can be pretty long on the North Coast. And I won't be able to afford to buy anywhere decent, not for a while, until I get a proper maintenance thing sorted with Derek. Me and Denzil will be stuck in one of Joanne's holiday homes that she rents out. Obviously nobody wants them in the winter. Sitting here listening to the wind howling. And I might be tempted . . . to go crawling back. But now I never, ever can. Because I broke every single damn window. And though Derek's not close with the neighbours, there's probably quite a few of them aware of the mess, by now. We've got the same cleaning lady as the ones on either side of us. Word'll not be long spreading. So there's no question of me going back. Ever ever ever.'

Vinny takes a deep breath.

'But . . . '

'What, you think I should have stayed?'

'No, I just . . . Where are you?'

Alex laughs. A harsh, gasping sort of laugh, but her face has gone back to its normal colour. She tosses her head, her earrings jangle.

'Have you really not got it yet? I'm in Portrush. At Joannne's place. Joanne, my sister. Where else would I have to go to?'

'But . . . what about Denzil?'

'Well, he's here. Obviously.'

'But what's he going to do?'

'Oh, you mean . . . School? The S word? Well, I got Joanne to ring the local, it's integrated, so . . . anyway there were no places left for P7 for next year, and I thought, oh God what have I done, and then I rang back myself. And I got the principal and she said there was only one place left. In P6. And I said Denzil's a June birthday, and I begged and pleaded with her and in the end she agreed; he's going into P6 in September.'

'P6? All over again?'

'No, really, he'll love it. He'll be telling the others what to do. And then maybe he can go to the integrated High School, in Coleraine, and he won't even have to sit the damn eleven-plus.'

She grins at Vinny. Triumphantly. Like a little girl who's been trailing dismally in all the races on Sports Day, and finally wins the obstacle race because all the others get stuck in the scramble net, except for her, because she's spotted a way through that no-one else noticed.

Then her cheeky grin fades, and she says 'But I'm really sorry about the money.'

'Money?'

'Yeah, you'll be losing at least fifty pounds a week. From now till November.'

'Oh Lord, don't worry about that,' Vinny says.

'I can't be forever making money out of somebody else's stress and misery.'

'Well, plenty of people do,' says Alex soberly.

They look at each other for a long, thoughtful moment. Behind Alex's head, the sky has lost its brightness; the sea has turned a soft grey. Alex opens the window; Vinny can hear a dog barking, somewhere close, and in the distance seagulls screaming. The wind is getting up, and the waves aren't exactly crashing, it's a softer noise than that, a sort of grumble in the distance.

'See what I mean? That wind can be pretty fierce, and this is supposed to be the summer. Oh they'll all come up and see us, Chloe and Stewart and their pals, but in the winter it's going to be pretty damn quiet.'

'I guess the trains still run in the winter,' Vinny says. 'And they're not that expensive. Roisin and I could come up, the odd time.'

'Bless you,' says Alex softly.

Vinny draws a deep breath and asks urgently, as if this question needs to be settled for once and for all, 'Alex, did you leave Derek because of Denzil? Or because of you?'

But suddenly here's Roisin, galloping up the stairs and into the room, waving a bit of paper, crowing 'Look, it's our plan! Me and the veg man! For the garden! Only he put in too much veg, I had to scribble some of it out and make a new plan.'

Alex grins. 'Show me. Hold it up to the screen – no, a bit closer – yeah, great plan, I see you're going to have a badminton net . . . '

'Not at all,' says Roisin. 'It's for volleyball. Crystal and Zoe both play volleyball.' She turns to Vinny accusingly. 'I'm hungry. Is there anything?'

Vinny says that there are potato waffles and sausages, Roisin can make a start, but she will have to persuade the veg man to stay and help her cook them, she is not to mess with hot fat on her own. Roisin beams.

'Sausages!' she thrusts the bit of paper at Vinny and pounds off down the stairs.

'She's got over it already,' Alex says. 'Shut up, Jasper – sorry, it's barking in my ear, I can't hear myself think – Well, maybe not got over, but started to move on—'

'Yeah. She's too big to climb in that rhododendron any more. And hide and seek will soon be just too childish for words. They grow up so quickly, don't they?'

'Yup, don't they just. And what about you?'

'Me . . . '

A crescendo of barks. Something large and hairy hurls itself across the screen.

'Vinny, I'm going to have to take this damn beast for a walk. It's an Irish wolfhound, Denzil can't manage it on his own. skype tomorrow?'

'Of course,' Vinny says, and as Alex waves and disappears from the screen, she feels all the muscles of her face relax.

For the last few minutes she's been unconsciously holding everything taut in a determined, encouraging smile. Now it can all just flop down. She gazes dumbly at the screen. Alex has forgotten to switch off the skype, and there's the window still slightly open, with its view of plain beige sand and sea which seems to change, even as she watches, from grey to deep violet blue and back to grey again, as a cloud passes over the sun. She can still hear the wind, and the dog barking, more distantly now, and seagulls. And an insistent, rather shrill *croo croo croo croo*. It's surely a pigeon, but what would a pigeon be doing on a beach?

The noise is actually coming from behind her. It's a pigeon, on her own windowsill; not a wood pigeon, but one of those urban ones, dark slatey grey with a bit of a sheen on its feathers. It regards her with a satirical eye, and as she makes a shooing motion, it flaps disdainfully away.

She is careful not to look out of the window. She swivels round on her office chair, yawns, rubs her eyes. Opens up the slightly crumpled bit of paper Roisin had thrust at her, and stares at it. There is the lawn, the volleyball net, the new, small apple trees, the rows of carrots and potatoes, all carefully labelled in Roisin's neat handwriting.

And then, all across one side, there's a mess. A mess in several different colours, loopy, straggly lines occasionally bursting out into scratchy-looking blossom, curling and rambling and twining, it doesn't take too much imagination to see in this scribble the flourishing mass of vegetation spilling out of the Hobgoblin's Hat.

And in what is obviously not Roisin's handwriting, and therefore must be Chris's, she reads:

Three-year plan. Rowan and birch saplings. Transplant ivy shoots? Lure birds in to excrete blackberry and sweet amber seeds? And beside it, in purple capitals: VINNY'S WILDERNESS.

It's not quite finished, she thinks. In the middle of the mess, using one of Roisin's felt tips that were lying beside the computer, she starts to draw a tree; but it's not a sapling, it comes out thick and solid like the dead rowan tree that was beside her terrace, the one she'd written the poem about. By the time it's old enough to be dead and grown with ivy, she thinks, I'll be dead myself . . .

She throws the window wide open, closes her eyes, leans out, feels the damp air cool on her face. Is that a blackbird or a wren singing somewhere, liquid and shrill and assertive, perched on a bush in someone else's garden, even though her own bushes are gone? Perhaps Chris would know? Thinking of Chris, she remembers again what he'd said about the teenage swifts, and suddenly she can hear them, a thin, high shrieking in the distance. She opens her eyes and there they are, tiny black crescents far above the garden, wheeling and swooping and screaming, showing off, as if the whole sky is their home.